WOLF BORN

LUNAR ACADEMY, YEAR ONE

ALYSSA ROSE IVY

JENNIFER SNYDER

Cover Design: Najla Qambar Designs

 Created with Vellum

RYAN

I should have shaved. I felt the stubble on my chin and realized my mom would kill me when she got the first-year pictures. Like everything else at Lunar Academy, new student pictures couldn't be retaken. You got one shot at everything. No exceptions. Kind of like every moment of my life. But luckily I was pretty damn good at doing things right the first time.

I heaved my large duffel out of the back of my truck and put it over my shoulder before I made my way to the large stone dormitory that would be my home for the next four years.

I made it less than ten steps before being stopped in my tracks.

"Hey, Ryan!" Lauren flipped her long brown hair off her shoulder. She had her hand on her hip in a posed way. Lauren was one of those girls who was always ready for a picture. "You finally made it."

"Hey." I pretended to be happy to see her. I didn't

really have a choice. Our families had been allies for generations. It wasn't changing no matter how annoying she could be.

"Can you believe it? We're finally here?" She played with a few strands of her hair.

"It is kind of crazy, but I'm ready." At least in principle I was. I could have handled a few more weeks of summer first. Or more than a few.

"Of course you are." She inclined her head to the side. That motion held way more symbolism than when a human did it. She knew what she was doing, but I refused to acknowledge it. "When aren't you ready?"

I smiled automatically without really feeling it. "Never."

I glanced around. The quad was mostly empty. I was even later than I thought. Not a huge deal, but I didn't have time to waste chatting with Lauren.

"That's what I love about you, Ryan. Your humility."

"Like you have any?" I threw it right back at her. I knew she could take it. I had to at least give her that.

"Touché." She took a step closer to me.

"I better get going." I adjusted my duffel on my back and headed toward the tables in front of the dormitory.

"We're headed to the same place." Lauren caught up with me. "Obviously, we're both in Wolf Born."

"Obviously." There was only one house for us. "Where's all your stuff? I don't believe for a second you only brought that bag." I nodded at the small purse she wore slung over her shoulder. It maybe could have held a phone and lipstick.

"Very funny. I had one of my parents' servants bring it to my room. Did you know Alaina and I got the large suite?"

"Shocking." I sped up.

"As if you aren't predictable. I'm sure your roommate is Finn."

"And your point?" I turned to look at her despite not wanting to. Sometimes it was better to engage in a conversation in order to finish it.

"I'm merely pointing out that my family isn't the only one who can pull strings."

"Who in Wolf Born can't pull strings?" There were four houses at the Lunar Academy, but Wolf Born had the largest amount of old-line families—it was hard not to. We were the pure-bloods born into what we were. Sure the Wolf Bounds had magic, and the Wolf Bloods were part vampire, but they didn't come from the stock we did. And don't even get me started on the Wolf Bittens...

"Not everyone can." She nodded toward the twins. Nadia and North were currently checking in at the table. Nadia was small for a wolf, tall, but slender in a way few of our kind were. North didn't share her slender build, but both tended to keep to themselves from what I'd been able to tell from the social events over the years.

"She's got like one suitcase with her. And you know they don't have servants." Lauren did nothing to hide the disdain in her voice.

"Who cares?" I had grown tired of Lauren already. Too bad I'd be spending the next four years in the same dorm as her. I headed to check in right as the twins disappeared inside the large hall.

"Ah, Mr. Grayson. I was wondering when you would get here." The woman sitting at the desk needn't have introduced herself. It was no mere administrator helping us sign in. It was one of the highest ranking professors in the house: Professor Blair. She'd been at Lunar Academy since before my parents were students. She looked nice, but I knew enough about her reputation to know better than to underestimate her.

"Hello, Professor Blair." I bowed my head marginally. "I apologize for the tardiness."

Her expression didn't change in the slightest: serious and bored. "Can the fake politeness, Mr. Grayson. I can see right through it."

"All right, then." Forget starting off on the right foot with her. "Where do I go next?"

"Go on up to the fourth floor and drop your stuff off. Your sidekick is already up there. Then get your picture taken for your ID and the house wall."

"You mean Finn?" I assumed she had to have meant my best friend.

"Who else could I possibly mean?" She yawned. Yes. Definitely bored.

Lauren giggled behind me.

"Hello, Ms. Addison." Professor Blair spoke in the same bored tone. At least it wasn't just me. "You finally ready to check in?"

I didn't wait for Lauren. Instead, I headed straight inside the two large doors of Wolf Born Hall.

I didn't linger downstairs. Pictures and awards littered the walls, but I didn't pause to admire them. They would just be a reminder of what was expected of me—perfection. I could pull it off, but I also wanted to enjoy my four years of college. After graduation, I'd be working for my parents twenty-four hours a day just like my older brothers.

I took the four flights quickly and entered the boys' side of the floor. I found my room all the way at the end. The full moon with my name and Finn's was a dead giveaway. As Professor Blair had already told me, Finn had beat me in. We hadn't taken the large boys suite for our year. Someone else requested it, and I told my parents not to worry about it. I didn't plan to spend a lot of time in my room anyway.

"Hey, man." Finn lay sprawled across his bed. Noticeably, he had selected the bed farthest from the window. He may have been my best friend, but he understood hierarchy.

"Hey. I can't believe you're unpacked already." I glanced at his dresser. Clothes were sticking out of the drawers, so I was using the term unpacked loosely, but his bag was stowed.

"I thought I'd turn over a new leaf." He tossed a basketball up in the air and caught it.

"A new leaf?" I eyed the overflowing dresser. "I kind of doubt that."

"Watch and see, man. We're at the academy now. Anything can happen." He set aside the ball and spread out his arms.

"I'll watch. By the way, meet anyone new yet? The only ones still out there when I checked in were Lauren and the twins."

He laughed. "You know Lauren was waiting for you."

I'd gathered that by the way she immediately approached me. "I don't know why."

"Yes, you do." He lay back down and propped himself up with his hands behind his head.

"Okay. I know why, but eventually she's got to understand nothing will ever happen with us." Sure, she was pretty, but that didn't make up for her bad attitude.

"Maybe she'll run to me, then. She's hot. You have to admit that."

"I admit nothing." I unzipped my duffel and pulled out my sheets. The standard dorm-issued ones already on the bed were scratchy, and who the hell knew who else had used them? "What time is the picture?" Maybe I had time to shave.

"We should probably go. We wouldn't want to miss our chance to get immortalized on the house wall."

"You know my parents would kill me if I screwed that up." Appearances were everything to my family—appearances and power. Power was something too.

"Yes, they'd skewer you. But then again, they'd do the same thing to me for letting it happen."

"They know you don't control me." No one controlled me aside from them.

"Yeah, but that doesn't change anything." He jumped up. "They'd still blame me."

"In that case..."

There was a knock on the door even though it was open. North Hazel stood there with a frown. "I've been told to get you for pictures."

"Why'd they ask you to do that?" Finn pulled on his shoes.

"I don't know. Does it matter?" North's frown grew. The guy was perpetually in a bad mood.

"Not really. Just not sure how you got stuck with the job." Finn was being his classic self. If he had a question, no matter how stupid it was, he asked it.

"Me neither." North turned and walked away.

"Weird kid." Finn shook his head.

"Yeah, I guess." I didn't think his reaction was weird. Just typical.

"Nadia got really hot though." Finn grinned.

"You think everyone is hot."

"I'm serious. You don't agree?"

"I didn't really see her. It was from a distance and just the back of her."

"I could make a joke there." He waggled an eyebrow.

"But you won't." I really wasn't in the mood, and any joke he'd make wouldn't be funny.

"Fine. I won't."

I gave up on unpacking for the time being and headed out the door. "Lock up behind you."

"Giving orders now?" Finn shifted his weight from foot to foot.

"You're last out."

"You would have said the same thing even if I was first."

"I'm not that lazy." I walked through the doorway.

"It has nothing to do with laziness." He followed and closed the door behind him.

I ignored the comment. I knew exactly what he meant. I also knew he would lock up.

We made it down the four flights of stairs to find a big group waiting.

"Finally, Mr. Grayson and Mr. Temple have decided to grace us with their presence." Professor Blair looked just as happy to see me this time.

I looked over the group. I recognized at least half of them. Another few I thought I'd seen at one event or another, and the rest I'd never laid eyes on before.

I was getting all sorts of looks. My guess was even the ones I didn't recognize recognized me. Lauren was standing with her best friend, Alaina, and they weren't hiding what was on their mind.

"Everyone else has finished their individual pictures. If you two latecomers would have yours taken, then we can get on to the group photo."

I took my picture, followed by Finn. My mom would be pissed about my stubble, but she'd get over it. At least I hadn't missed the picture completely.

I automatically went toward the back row for the picture. Someone walked into me. I looked down. It was Nadia.

"Sorry," she mumbled without glancing at my face.

I took a good look at her. Finn wasn't wrong. There was something different about her. Was it her hair? No. It was still as long and curly as always. Something else? The more I studied her the more I realized it wasn't just one thing. It was everything. Maybe I just hadn't really looked at her before.

"No. It's my fault." I waited for her to look up at me. She'd have to catch my eye eventually.

"What? Ryan Grayson taking the blame?" Lauren laughed.

A kid I didn't recognize echoed her laugh.

I forced a smile, doing my part for the picture, before glaring at the kid again. "Do you have a problem?"

"No." He put a hand in his back pocket. "I just laugh when things are funny."

"And you are?" Lauren grazed her lip between her teeth. She made her flirting so obvious it wasn't even funny.

"Dameon Miles. Pleasure to meet you, Lauren." He took her hand and kissed it.

She blushed. Lauren freaking blushed. "How do you know my name?"

"Unlike the rest of you, I did my research." He released her hand, and his eyes set on Nadia next. He didn't say anything, but she noticed and looked in the other direction.

"What region are you from?" Lauren took a step to the right to effectively block Nadia from his view.

"Can't you tell from my accent?" He wasn't looking at Lauren anymore. He'd stepped around her and was looking at Nadia again.

"The UK. I don't know whose territory though." Nadia put her chin in her hand.

Dameon gave a barely noticeable nod. "Any other questions?"

"All the way over there. Yet you are here. Why not go to school over the pond instead?" I didn't give a damn how rude I came across. Something about this guy got under my skin.

"I wanted to go here. I met the qualifications. Why not?" He made complete eye contact. I wasn't used to dudes doing that. It was almost disarming—but it wasn't. Nothing disarmed me.

"Well, we're glad you're here." Alaina put her arm around Lauren's waist. "Aren't we, Lauren?"

"Very." Lauren reached out and ran a hand down his chest.

Finn laughed.

Lauren rolled her eyes at him, and then shifted her full attention back to Dameon. "We are both glad indeed." Her tongue snaked out to moisten her lips.

Maybe I'd finally get Lauren off my back. This guy might not be so bad after all. Then, I heard it. A tiny snicker. I looked over to see Nadia trying to cover her face.

"Ryan?" Lauren snapped.

"Huh?" I pulled my eyes away from Nadia.

"I was just telling Dameon that you'll be president of our year." Lauren's gaze moved back and forth between us.

"Oh." Already worried about that stuff? "I guess I probably will."

"There hasn't been an election yet." Dameon

stretched out his arms like he was readying for a fight. "We'll see. I heard they don't even have it until second semester for first years."

"An election?" Finn raised an eyebrow. "Right."

I eyed Dameon. I didn't particularly care about being president, but I did mind some outsider thinking he could step into my place. My parents would kill me if that happened. "Whatever you say, David."

"It's Dameon." He frowned, deep lines setting in around his face.

"My bad." This guy was seriously getting on my nerves. It was best I walked away while I still had control.

NADIA

*R*yan had a challenger. I hadn't seen that coming. This would make for an interesting distraction. No one back home would have dreamed of challenging a Grayson. But we weren't back home. Not that being at Lunar Academy really changed things. He was still a Grayson, and that meant he could get away with anything.

"Hey, Nadia." Ryan called my name as I made my way to the dining hall. "Wait up."

After a beat, I stopped and turned around. "Hi." We'd probably spoken a dozen times in our lives, which meant I wasn't exactly on his radar.

I wasn't sure why I was now.

"Some great company we have this year, huh?" He nodded toward the group still congregated in the lobby.

"Eh, just more of the same."

"Oh." He seemed to consider his answer. "I guess so."

I tucked a few strands of hair behind my ear. I had no

idea what to say. He must need something. Otherwise, he wouldn't be talking to me. I wished he would just spit it out.

"Well, just saying hi. I guess I'll see you at dinner." He gave a half wave and walked off ahead of me.

I blinked. What?

"What did he want?" North caught up with me. He didn't hide the venom in his voice.

"Nothing. At least he didn't seem to." I was still trying to figure out what that was about.

"You need to stay away from guys like that, Nadia. You're too smart for those games."

"You think I don't know that?" Anger flashed through me.

"No. I know you do. But it never hurts to remind you." North stuffed his hands in his pockets.

"One of these days you'll stop worrying about me."

"Yeah. When I'm dead," he mumbled.

"North, you are being an idiot."

"I'm your big brother. It's my job to look out for you." He looked down and a lock of unruly brown hair fell into his face, partially blocking his eyes. Combine his hairstyle with his all black garb, if North didn't look like an emo kid, nobody did.

"You were born two minutes before me. We've been over this. That doesn't really make you my big brother."

"I was born before you. That means I'm older. What seems to be the problem?"

"Forget it, North. Just forget it." I felt around to make sure I had my student ID in my pocket. It would take me a while to get used to carrying it with me, but since it was my meal ticket and the key to my room, I'd better get used to it soon.

"You're the one contradicting something factual."

"Is there a reason you came over here to talk to me?" I felt like I was having a repeat of my conversation with Ryan. There was comfort in the quiet. I preferred it. I was already worried that my best friend, Jackie, hadn't shown up yet. We'd decided early on to be roommates, and I couldn't imagine why she wasn't here already. It was unlike her. She was never late to anything. My teeth sank into my bottom lip. Hopefully, she'd just gotten held up.

"I still think we should have pushed harder to stay out of this place." North slowed his long-legged pace so we could walk together. At five feet seven inches, I was short for a wolf, but tall compared to most human girls. If it weren't for our family's name, no one would have believed I belonged in the Wolf Born house.

I sighed. "This is where we need to be." This wasn't the first time he'd broached the subject.

"Why? I mean what do they teach here that we couldn't teach ourselves?"

"You didn't have to come." I'd told him this on more than one occasion.

"Sure I did. We stick together. Just as we always have." His eyes bore into mine. "And we always will."

"One day you will have to accept that I can take care of my myself." I softened my voice. I didn't want to insult him, but he needed to let go. I might not be the strongest wolf physically, but I was smarter than just about anyone. I had great reflexes, and I could dodge trouble. I didn't like to run from my problems, but sometimes it was the only way.

"I've never doubted you can do that."

"Yeah?" It was my turn to raise an eyebrow.

"You just trust too much." He veered to the right as we neared the student center that housed the dining hall. "You want to see the good in everyone."

I laughed so hard I snorted. "Right."

"You do. Whether you want to admit it or not."

"Don't you have somewhere else to be?" I was about to lose my cool, and that wouldn't be good for either of us.

"Sure. Home."

"This is our home August through May for the next four years. Might as well get used to it."

"I guess so." He shrugged.

"I'm hungry. Come if you want. If you'd rather mope, you're doing it alone." I headed through the student center doors.

I walked right over to the buffet line. From what I'd heard, the food was supposed to be decent, but it was also meat heavy. Most wolves liked meat. I wasn't like most wolves. I wasn't a full vegetarian, but I went for the more plant-based options when given a chance. Not to mention, my way of eating helped me steer clear of the blood that might attract the Wolf Bloods. Those half-vampires made me nervous.

I found a few options beyond the salad bar and took a seat at an empty table. Without needing to look, I knew

North had sat down next to me. His tray hit the table with a thump, sending fries scattering everywhere.

I eyed the giant cheeseburger in front of him. Admittedly, it smelled kind of good.

"Enjoy your rabbit food, sis." He picked up his burger and took a bite.

"I will. Thank you very much." I took a nice bite of my salad. At least the academy got fresh produce. I'd learned not to correct his rabbit food comments; it always ended with him explaining that evolutionarily our kind needed meat. And then I'd go into the fact that we weren't really wolves, but instead hybrids and therefore completely different. Neither of us ever changed the other's mind, so it was really a waste of time to hash it out. Again.

"Hello, fellow Wolf Borns. Mind if I join you?" Dameon stood across the table from us.

"Uh, sure." The dining hall was open to everyone, and I didn't own the table. Plus, it wasn't like there was anyone else we were saving the seats for.

"North and Nadia. Right?" He sprinkled an inordinate amount of salt on top of his fries.

I set my fork down. "I don't believe we were formally introduced."

"We didn't need to be." Dameon smiled. "I already knew."

"Uh, because that isn't sketchy?"

North raised an eyebrow at me. "It's not sketchy."

After his whole you-can't-trust-people talk, he was playing things that way?

"Is everything okay?" Dameon looked between us.

"Yeah. Everything is fine." North shot me a look. "Just siblings discussing things."

"Twins are extremely really rare for wolves." Dameon bit into one of his fries.

"We know." I'd heard that line more than a few times before.

"Which means you two are special."

"Rare does not necessarily equal special." For some reason people struggled to understand that.

"Sure it does." Dameon picked up his burger. "You two are very special."

"I knew we liked you." North grinned.

I glared at him. Why was he grinning at this guy? He never grinned. What the hell was going on here? I laughed dryly. "Really?" I pushed back my chair.

"You've barely touched your food." Dameon pointed to my tray.

"I've lost my appetite." I'd have to get something from the vending machine I'd noticed in the dormitory lounge later.

"Wait. I promise I'll make this worth your time."

"Make what worth my time?" I hesitated with my tray in my hands.

Dameon pushed his chair back from the table. "An alliance."

"An alliance?" I repeated the words. "Why would we need an alliance?"

"Are you really asking that question?" He raised both eyebrows.

"Yes, I am really asking it."

"I'd have thought a girl as smart as you would know the answer to that." His lips twisted into a smirk.

"Pretend I'm not smart."

He leaned forward and lowered his voice. "You haven't sensed it?"

"Sensed what?" My skin prickled with unease.

"Run with me tonight." He looked between us. "Both of you. I can show you."

"I'll pass." I wasn't buying whatever he was selling. "But North can do what he wants." I walked away to dump my tray even though wasting food made me cringe.

I glanced at the other tables on my way out the door and caught Ryan's eye. He looked momentarily surprised before he raised an eyebrow in greeting.

Weird first day.

As soon as the sun set, I headed outside. I had no interest in running with Dameon or breaking an academy rule, but I didn't trust the guy enough to leave North on his own with him during a run. He may technically be my older brother, but that didn't mean I couldn't protect him.

The Lunar Academy strictly forbid shifting unless part of a sanctioned group, so by following I was about to break a rule on the first night. It didn't bother me nearly as much as it should have. I was far more afraid of something happening to North, or more likely, him getting into a huge mess he couldn't get out of.

Still, I hesitated at the edge of the woods, trying to come up with an alternative plan—any other sort of plan —besides having to shift. But I came up empty. Shifting and running was all there was. This was the only way to catch up to them fast enough.

Well, if I was breaking a rule, at least I would enjoy it.

I reached out for my wolf, loving the surge of power that came with letting her take over. My vision tunneled as my dominant form set in. And I ran.

It didn't take long to catch North's scent. It was the first scent I'd ever learned, and it was by far the easiest one for me to follow. It was both similar to mine yet different. Kind of the way we were. I ran after it, careful to keep some distance. I immediately caught the second scent. Dameon was here too. His scent was strong, like black licorice. My wolf snarled. I fell back, slowing my wolf's pace. The last thing I wanted was for Dameon to catch me. I wouldn't let him think I cared at all about what he was into. I needed to stay invisible.

The woods flew by as I continued. I picked up my pace as we neared the border of the school grounds. It was one thing to be breaking the shifting rule on campus, but to leave campus entirely while shifted was not a risk I wanted to take.

North's trail continued ahead. The farther I ran, the more I worried about him. The fur on my back stood on end when I caught another scent. I wasn't alone. I debated my options. If I stopped, there was a good chance

I'd lose the trail. But if I kept going, I might get a surprise attack from behind. This might be a trap. I ran harder. If I were only following Dameon, I would have stopped, but North might be in danger. I pushed myself harder. I could feel the other wolf beside me now. I reached out and couldn't find North's scent. It was as if it had completely disappeared. But that was impossible.

I could feel the other wolf catching up to me. Before long, he or she would overtake me. I didn't care. I couldn't stop. I pushed harder and faster. Then, I lost my footing and tumbled down a slope. Damn it. Why was I being so clumsy? I recognized the dark, sweet scent before the wolf walked over. I hurried back to my wolf feet. It came as no surprise when the air shimmered and in the wolf's place stood a very naked, and far too sexy, Ryan.

"Hey. Shift back. I need to talk to you." Ryan was talking to me, but all I could do was ogle him. I was sick. What was I doing? Sure he was six feet of solid, and very sexy, muscle. That didn't mean I needed to stare at him. I was no better than Lauren. "Come on, Nadia. Fast."

I tried to find North's scent again, but there was nothing. Not even a trace of Dameon's sharp scent remained. I ignored Ryan and kept searching. They couldn't have disappeared into thin air, but I didn't see any other possibility. There was nothing here. Not even a disturbance in the leaves that covered the forest floor.

"Nadia, cut it out. Shift back. We need to talk." Ryan's expression was serious, and his tone matched.

Talk? What the heck could he possibly want to talk about? Did he know where North was? I ran behind some trees and shifted. I'd hidden my clothes back closer to the dorms. "What are you doing here?" I snapped. "How dare you follow me."

"How dare I?" He put a hand to his chest. His bare chest. "What? I can't run near you? Wolves are supposed to run in packs, you know."

"Sure. But the two of us don't make a pack. Not to mention, it's against the rules to run without everyone else."

"Yet you're doing it."

"You didn't let me finish." I made sure to stay hidden behind the trees. "Second, the woods are huge. You were running right next to me. Were you following me?"

"Following you? Because you aren't full of yourself." He rubbed the back of his neck.

"You know what I mean." The conversation was getting old, and I needed to find North. "And why don't you get dressed? Or shift back to your wolf."

"What? What is your issue with nudity? We're wolves."

"Yes. But that doesn't mean I want you seeing me naked."

"Unfortunately, I'm not seeing you naked right now." He grinned.

"Yes, but I'm seeing you, so it's still a problem."

"For you maybe. Not for me." He winked.

"Answer me, then." I averted my eyes from his lower half. I really didn't need to see how big that part of his anatomy was.

"Answer what? Why I'm naked?"

"No. Get over the naked bit. If you want to stay naked, be my guest, but don't flatter yourself by thinking it does anything for me." Technically, a lie. It was doing a whole lot for me, but nothing I would act on.

"Yeah?" His grin grew. "I'm a wolf, Nadia. You think I can't smell your arousal?"

Damn. He had me there.

"Okay. Shut up." I could feel the blood rushing to my face. "Cover yourself then answer me."

He laughed. "I don't think I've ever seen you so flustered."

"I don't think I've ever seen you be such a jerk." We were wasting time. "Yes. I have, but why were you following me?"

"I wasn't following you. I was following Dameon."

His expression seemed open and honest. Was I being stupid? Maybe he wasn't following me at all. Embarrassment hit me. "Okay. We were doing the same thing." Not that it mattered. The trail was completely cold.

"What the hell was your brother doing out here with him?"

"What makes you think I know?"

"He's your brother. Don't you two tell each other everything?"

"Just because we're siblings doesn't mean we tell each other everything." We used to, but it had been years since North had really confided in me. To be fair, it had also been years since I'd confided in him. Somewhere along the line, we'd slowly began to drift apart.

"You're not just siblings. You're twins."

I groaned. "What is it with everyone and their obsession with us being twins?"

"Everyone?" Ryan's brows pinched together. "Who else has been talking about that?"

"No one. I mean generally." I didn't want him thinking I was obsessing over Dameon—or to give away my hunch that he wanted North and I involved in something serious. The talk of allies had unnerved me.

"Nuh uh." Ryan shook his head. "You don't get to toss that comment to the side. You're talking about someone specific, aren't you?"

"Drop it. It doesn't matter. Let's stick to what's important."

"And what's that?" Ryan was so at ease standing around naked. I should have felt that way too, but I didn't. I never had.

Sometimes I wished I could be like normal wolves.

"Why Dameon is out here."

Ryan's gaze drifted to the woods around us before coming back to rest on me. "Also, why is North out here with him? Come clean with me."

I thought about my options. I didn't totally trust Ryan, but I trusted him more than I trusted Dameon. That had to count for something. "He wanted to show us something. There was also talk of making an alliance."

"An alliance?" Ryan's forehead furrowed. "Why?"

I sighed. "If I knew, would I be standing out here like this?"

"Where the hell did they go?" He looked deeper into

the woods. "I had their scent, and then there was nothing."

"You witnessed the same thing I did."

His brows pinched tight as his gaze swept over the surrounding area again. "They couldn't have disappeared. They lost us somehow. We need to find them. We have to run."

"You mean shift back?" I scoffed. "Why did you make me shift in the first place?"

"Aren't you the one who is in a rush?" He shifted right there in front of me.

I waited a moment and did the same.

It was getting late. Really late. And the number of rules we were violating was growing. Yet there I went. Running deeper into the woods with Ryan Grayson. Less than twenty-four hours at the Lunar Academy, and I'd completely lost my mind.

RYAN

This was insane. I was running through the woods with Nadia Hazel, trying to find her brother and Dameon—who was easily the most annoying wolf I'd ever met, and who I was now stuck dealing with for the next four years.

Nadia was fast, but I had to keep my pace slower than normal to stay at her side. I didn't mind, as we had absolutely no clue where we were going other than following the faint whiff of a scent. Or why we were even running. We'd shifted back to our wolves so fast that we hadn't even discussed what we'd do if we found them.

I tried to focus on the more pressing matter of finding the others, but my thoughts kept going back to the teasing glimpse of skin I'd seen through the trees. And the smell of arousal. Nadia was into me whether she admitted it or not. How hadn't I noticed her before?

Nadia stopped short. I did the same, watching as she sniffed at something in the leaves. The scent tickled my nose as a slight breeze kicked up. It was a strange scent. Definitely wolf, but tinged with something else too.

A noise in the distance caught my attention. Was that a bell? Shit. That couldn't be a good thing. With a quick glance at each other, we turned around and headed back to campus. Once again, I slowed my pace to match hers. Maybe she wouldn't have cared if I left her behind, but I did.

Something strange had happened back there.

We were nearly back to the edge of the woods when I noticed a figure standing there. Nadia stopped short. The figure started to wave his hands and walk toward us. Finn?

I shifted back to my human form.

"Dude, what the hell are you thinking?" Finn held out clothes to me. "Get changed. Fast."

Nadia stood stone still in wolf form.

Finn nodded. "Ah. I take it these are yours?" He held out a tank top and shorts.

She used her mouth to pull them from his hand and then ran off. No doubt for privacy.

I was dressed by the time she came back. Admittedly, I would've liked to have watched her change so I could catch a glimpse of her body, but the whole tank top without a bra thing she had going on was working for her. It made it easy to fill in the blanks.

"So, which one of you wants to tell me what's going on?" Finn looked between us.

"What was that sound?"

"What sound?" Finn glared at me like I'd gone nuts.

"It was like a bell. I only heard it once or twice, but it was loud." Nadia described the same thing I'd heard.

"I didn't hear a bell." Finn looked over his shoulder. "Were you guys taking something?"

"Don't be ridiculous. There was a bell. How did you not hear it?" She looked over at me. "Tell him there was a bell, Ryan."

"There was a bell." Or something like one. I'd definitely heard something.

"Okay. So you were running in the woods together hearing bells?" Finn rolled his eyes. "Right."

"What are you doing out here?" He still hadn't explained his presence.

"What am I doing out here?" He laughed dryly. "Is that a joke?"

"No, it's not." Nadia put a hand on her hip. "You asked us, only fair that you'd be willing to tell us too."

"I'm trying to make sure Ryan doesn't get expelled on his first day."

"He couldn't get expelled if he tried," Nadia snapped. "So moving on..." she trailed off.

"I don't know if I'd go that far..." Sure my name got me some leeway, but it also made me a target. There were some messes even my parents couldn't get me out of.

Finn looked back toward the Wolf Born dormitory before shifting his gaze back to us. "Just tell me what you guys were up to."

"It's a long story." And one that needed to wait.

"It's a long story my ass," Finn snapped.

"Finn. Seriously."

"What? I'm out here risking my neck for you. Like I always do. The least you can do is fill me in."

I looked around. "Fine. But not here."

"There's nothing to tell." Nadia clenched her jaw. "Might as well head inside though."

"Okay, which is it?" Finn groaned. "A long story, or nothing to tell?"

"Fine. Come with me." I led the way back to the Wolf Born dormitory and used my card to get us in.

We looked behind us before we slipped inside and let the door click closed behind us. At first glance, the lobby was empty, but there was a small scraping sound somewhere nearby. Nadia grabbed an arm of each of us and towed us back behind the stairs.

Finn grinned at me. I couldn't help but return it. For such a little wolf, she sure knew how to take charge. I wondered if she was also like that in bed.

My thoughts were interrupted by the sound of footsteps coming from the lounge.

"Remember, don't tell anyone." Dameon stepped into view. I was almost positive he could see us, but if he did, he didn't show it.

"Why would I tell anyone?" North looked around. Did he sense Nadia's presence?

"How did they get back here before us?" I asked even though I assumed they didn't have the answer. It made no sense. Wouldn't we have seen them on our way back?

"Shh!" Nadia hissed.

"We're not alone. Let's go." Dameon headed for the stairs with North right behind him.

"Follow me." Nadia moved to the back wall and started to run her hands over it. Nothing happened at first, but then there was the faint sound of gears turning, and a seam appeared in the wall. She slipped her fingers inside the small gap and revealed a narrow doorway.

"What the hell is this?" Finn asked.

"Keep it down," Nadia hissed.

"Where the hell are you taking us?" Finn asked.

She stepped through the door. "Shh."

I followed.

Finn pulled back on my shoulder. "Come on, man. Don't you want to make sure she isn't taking us to a dungeon? Wait. Maybe that wouldn't be so bad."

"Do you want me to deck you?" Nadia barely glanced over her shoulder as she spat the words.

"Shh. You aren't supposed to be talking, remember?" I tossed back to her as I followed her down a spiral staircase.

She continued down the stairs, ignoring me. When we reached the bottom, she turned toward Finn and me. "We can talk now."

"Where the hell are we?" Finn looked around at the empty room. The floors were a rough stone, nothing like the polished floors above. The walls were the same material, and the only light came from faint rays seeping in from a mostly blocked window.

Nadia rolled her shoulders back. "We are in an old interrogation room. It's not even on the maps anymore."

"Uh... and why are we here?" Finn backed away from her. "Because I really don't want to die."

"We're here because it's soundproof, and I'm probably the only one who knows it's here." Nadia spread her arms wide. "It's mostly forgotten."

"I'll repeat. I really don't want to die."

Nadia sighed. "Quit being so dramatic, Finn."

"So why did we need to go someplace soundproof?" That was the question Finn should have been asking.

"And how do you know it's soundproof?" Finn rubbed his chin. "You're kind of creeping me out."

"I know because I always do my research."

"And, did you do your research on Dameon?" He was why we'd both been out in the woods.

"I didn't know he was coming." She looked down. "I did look at the list of incoming students, and as of a few weeks ago, he wasn't on there."

"Seems like you aren't as good at research as you like to make it sound."

I punched Finn's arm.

He rubbed his arm. "Hey."

"Stay focused. You said you wanted to hear. Listen."

"All I heard was talk about research."

He was right. We couldn't stay down in this room forever. Eventually, we needed to get to the point. "We were out there following Dameon and North."

"Why?" Finn leaned against the banister.

"Because I don't trust the guy." I hadn't from the moment I met him.

"What he said." Nadia pointed to me.

I glanced at her. "Are you actually agreeing with me?"

"Yes. Yes, I am." She gave the smallest hint of a smile.

"Okay." Finn narrowed his eyes. "Why are you two arguing like you're sleeping together?"

"What?" Nadia blanched. "That's not even funny."

"Who said it was funny?" Finn crossed his arms. "It's the truth."

"It's not." Nadia shook her head. "But whatever. It's late. We need to talk so we can actually get some sleep."

"Sleep?" I didn't bother to hide my surprise. "You're thinking about sleep at a time like this?"

"Yes. We can't possibly be at our best if we don't sleep."

"Whatever you say." Sleep was the last thing on my mind. We had too many questions—namely where did North and Dameon disappear to in the woods, and how did they get back so fast? "Let's get down to it. As I was saying, we followed Dameon and North. Then we lost their scent. We tried to find them again. When we got back, they were already here. Makes no sense."

"Here's an idea." Finn put a finger to his temple. "Go ask North. He is Nadia's brother after all."

Nadia groaned. "Why do you think it would be easy for me to just ask my brother?"

"Because it should be." Finn yawned. He wasn't the type to get tired, so I assumed he was trying to emphasize he was bored.

"Okay. So if it's dangerous, he'll probably lie to keep me away." Nadia put a hand on her hip. "Simple as that."

"And if it's not dangerous, he'll tell you they went out for a beer or hot dogs?" Finn suggested.

"Hot dogs?" Nadia wrung her hands at her side. "Can you be serious for a minute?"

"What?" Finn grinned. "Doesn't that sound good to you guys?"

I decided Finn's joke didn't need a response. "I do think you need to ask him first. Even him lying will tip us off. And you can argue all you want, but you know when North is lying."

"True." Nadia nodded. "I do. I'll talk to him when I can. Until then, keep your mouths shut. We don't need anyone finding out about this. Especially not Dameon. He doesn't need to know we're suspicious."

"All right. Is it time to leave this dungeon, then?" Finn straightened.

"It's not a dungeon. It's an interrogation room." Nadia slipped past Finn and started up the stairs.

"Big difference," Finn mumbled.

We reached the top of the stairs and ended up back into the dark section behind the stairs. Nadia made a zipping motion over her lips.

Professor Blair turned the corner. "Excuse me? What are you three doing behind the stairs?"

"Uh." Generally, I was good at thinking on my feet, but for one reason or another, I completely blanked.

"These two were making out." Finn pointed a thumb at Nadia and me. "I was trying to break it up. You know, don't want either to do something they might regret."

Nadia scowled at him but didn't argue.

Professor Blair looked over at Nadia. "Ms. Hazel, I would think you would have better taste."

Nadia opened her mouth like she wanted to say something, but then she closed it again. Instead, she gave Finn and me a warning glance and hurried off.

"Mr. Grayson. A word please?" Professor Blair clasped her hands in front of her. "Mr. Temple, please excuse us and let us speak."

"Yes, ma'am." Finn mouthed good luck and made his way around the stairs.

"Is there something I can do for you, professor?" I wasn't sure why I was being singled out, but I figured it couldn't be a good thing.

"Yes. You can tell me what's really going on."

"Excuse me?" I knew this was coming, but I was trying to buy myself time. What possible excuse could I use, and how much did she know? Did she know we'd shifted? Did I reek of wolf and woods? There was nothing in the rules that said you couldn't make out behind the stairs.

"You expect me to believe that you convinced Ms. Hazel to meet with you behind the staircase? First of all, Ms. Hazel has better taste. Second, behind the stairs? This isn't junior high."

Once again, she brought up taste. In what world was I a bad choice as a mate for anyone? "Then why are you asking me? Shouldn't you be asking all of us?"

"I chose to ask you." She pointed at me. "So answer."

"Believe it or not, Nadia likes me. As to the location, it wasn't planned." Sticking with Finn's story sounded like the best option. Plus, maybe like was a stretch, but I happened to know for a fact Nadia was attracted to me.

"Mr. Grayson." Professor Blair frowned. "Might I counsel you to be careful. Your last name can't protect you from everything."

"Never said it could."

"You can believe plenty of things without saying a word out loud."

"True. Very true."

"Then we have an understanding?" She adjusted the sleeves on her robe.

"Yes. No more kissing Nadia under the stairs." I nodded. "We'll find another place."

She shook her head. "Good night, Mr. Grayson."

"Good night," I mumbled. My heart pounded. This was a way crazier first night than I could have ever imagined.

"And might I suggest really considering Ms. Hazel. She would be a formidable ally for you."

"Ally?" I turned around. That sounded entirely too close to alliance talk. Professor Blair was already slipping back outside.

I walked upstairs, ready to head to bed and put the night behind me, but I found North blocking my door.

"Can I help you?" I wanted to ask him a million more pressing questions, but I'd promised Nadia I wouldn't tip him off.

"Yes, you can." His face hardened. "Stay away from my sister."

"I don't know what you're talking about." As far as I knew, he hadn't seen or smelled us in the woods.

"Don't be an idiot." North scowled.

Finn strolled down the hall with a towel around his waist. His hand was on the edge of it, as if he was getting ready to use it as a weapon. For all our sakes, I hoped he didn't.

"You know exactly what I'm talking about." A muscle throbbed in North's neck.

"No, I don't." I wasn't admitting to anything.

"You might think this is a game, but it most certainly isn't."

"I don't play games." They were a waste of time, and in the end, almost everyone was a loser. Which was why I needed to completely change my tactic. Hopefully, Nadia didn't try to kill me for it. "I never play games. But you do."

"Excuse me?"

"What were you doing out there?" A side of my personality—the impatient part—was coming out.

"Why would that be any of your business?"

"Kind of how whatever happens between Nadia and me isn't your business either." I understood North was her brother, but that didn't mean I would let him push me around.

"I thought nothing happened." A smirk settled on his face.

"I never said it did. I said whatever happens. Future tense. Not present."

"But you are saying something will happen." Finn grinned. "I knew it."

I glared at him. "Go put some clothes on."

"That's what she said." He laughed.

"Finn." Hopefully, he understood this wasn't a joke.

"Fine, master. I shall do what you bid." With a bow, he disappeared into the room.

"That's sick, you know?" North nodded toward my now closed door.

"What is?"

"That you have your best friend calling you master. You're a conceited piece of work."

"That was a joke. I don't have him call me master."

"But you make him do whatever you want." North leaned against the wall.

"That's not entirely true." I didn't make Finn do anything. Did he listen most of the time? Yes. But most people listened to me.

"It is."

"He does what he wants."

"No, he doesn't." North straightened up.

My fists clenched at my sides. He was getting on my nerves. "Why do you even care?"

"Because I'm done sitting back and taking your crap."

"What crap have I ever given you?" I wasn't friends with the guy, but that didn't mean I'd ever been rude to him.

"Really? Going to play innocent on that too?"

"Stop it right now." Nadia marched down the hall.

"What are you doing here?" North's mouth fell open. "This is the boys' hall."

"I've broken enough rules tonight. Do you think this one will cause me much more trouble?" Nadia was looking at me when she answered. And I liked that. I really liked having her eyes on me.

"No. Probably not." I laughed. I'd had no idea what kind of balls the girl had—figuratively of course.

"Why are you laughing?" North scowled.

"Because she's right. She's totally right."

"If you're done laughing, Nadia must have a reason she's here." He crossed his arms.

"Where's Dameon?" Nadia looked down the empty hall.

"In his room probably." North shrugged.

"Which is where?" Nadia took a few steps down the hall.

"Room 412. That way." North pointed.

"Good. Let's go." She started down the hall.

"Wait. What?" Hadn't we just discussed keeping things quiet? How was this keeping anything quiet? Now I'd already broken that rule myself, but that didn't mean she should be confronting Dameon.

"Just follow. If you want." Nadia glanced at me over her shoulder. Unless I was imagining things, there was something else in that look. A look that went beyond shut up. She was up to something. And I'd play along. She was right. We'd already broken a lot of rules tonight. What was one more?

NADIA

Sometimes, scratch that, most of the time- when you wanted something done right, you needed to do it yourself. And sometimes, even if you wanted someone's help, the best solution was to pull them in with no warning. Hopefully Ryan was as smart as he was supposed to be, and he'd follow along.

I knocked on Dameon's door. I wasn't sure if he would answer though. If not, I was already formulating a plan B in my head.

Plan A worked. He pulled open the door wearing only his underwear. At least he was wearing underwear. "Yes?"

I kept my eyes firmly directed to his top half. And it wasn't a bad looking top half. The guy clearly worked out. He was no Ryan Grayson but—oh my God. I'd just compared a guy to Ryan Grayson as the standard of what was hot. "Can we talk?"

"Yes. We can talk. Come on in." He pulled the door

open wider. I was hit by the sound of jazz music. I hadn't been expecting that one.

I took a step inside. Ryan started to follow. "Nope. I said she should come on in. Not you."

"And me." North pushed his way around Ryan. "My sister isn't going into your room alone."

"North, do you really think I'd hurt your sister?" Dameon patted his shoulder. "You can rest assured she's safe with me."

I appreciated that he wasn't writing off my strength, but unfortunately, I wasn't the strongest wolf around. "I'll be fine." What I lacked in physical strength, I made up for in cunning. I'd be more than fine. Dameon was the one who needed to be careful.

"We'll be right here." Ryan caught my eye.

I nodded to let him know I understood he was staying close.

North glared at Ryan. "She's not your sister. It's not your job to protect her."

"No. She's *not* my sister." Ryan emphasized the word not. "And we can all be glad for that."

"I'll be fine." I didn't respond to his comment. Was he implying that I'd be a bad sister, or that he didn't think about me in that way at all? It didn't matter. It was time to get answers.

"If you gentleman will excuse us." Dameon closed the door.

I tried to ignore the slight worry that came over me when the door closed. I knew I could take care of myself, but that didn't mean I was comfortable being alone with this guy. This nearly naked guy.

"Make yourself comfortable." He gestured toward his bed.

I took a seat on his desk chair. "Would you mind putting some more clothes on?"

"Yes, I would mind." He laughed. "Just because you want to be uncomfortable, doesn't mean I have to be." He sprawled on his bed, with his hands behind his head. "This may take a while."

"I don't think it should take long at all." And I certainly didn't want it to.

"Oh? Is that so?" His eyes watched me with an intensity that unnerved me. "What can I do for you, Nadia?"

"Why do you keep saying my name? I'm the only one here."

"I like your name. When I like something, I take it in any way I can."

"That's not normal."

"Sure it is." He rolled onto his side. "At least it is for me."

"And that ups your creepy factor." This guy was something else.

"You say that like it's a bad thing."

And time to change the subject. "What happened out there tonight?"

"Wow. Straight to the chase."

"That's why I'm here."

"Are you sure that's why?"

"What other reason could I possibly have?"

"Well, I don't know." He ran his hand over the comforter beside him. "Maybe the unbelievable chemistry between us."

I laughed. "Right." The only one I had unbelievable chemistry with was Ryan, and I wasn't even sure what to do about that.

"I invited you tonight. Really it was your company I wanted, but I thought including North would make you more comfortable." He moved onto his back again. "My mistake."

"Yet, you took North anyway." Maybe saying no had been a mistake. If I'd gone, I wouldn't be asking questions now and I wouldn't have seen Ryan naked. It would have solved two of my problems at the same time.

"I did."

"That's it. That's your answer? You did?" Frustration welled up inside me. My wolf howled.

"Would you prefer a different answer?"

"Come on." I took a few deep breaths to calm myself. It was bad enough I was in a boy's room after curfew, adding shifting to that would only compound make my rule breaking.

"Join me over here, and I'll tell you anything you want to know."

I picked up a book and sent it directly toward his head. He caught it easily. "Wow. Easy there, tiger. I wouldn't want either of us getting hurt. Imagine having to explain to the administration why you were in my room this late."

I groaned. "Tell me what you were doing out there."

"First, tell me something." He crossed his legs at the ankles. That made me look at his legs. His muscular bare legs. Why did he insist on wearing only his underwear? This whole thing was utterly ridiculous.

"What?" I wasn't telling him anything, but I'd humor him if it served my goals.

"What do you know of Ryan Grayson?"

"What don't I know of him? He's a household name where I come from."

"He's a household name everywhere. Or rather his family is." Dameon sat up and took a small case off his bed stand. He pulled out a cigar. A freaking cigar. Who the hell was this kid?

"Then why are you asking me questions about him?"

"Because you know more than what people say." He chewed on the cigar.

"What makes you say that?"

"You're in the same circles, and you do your research."

"If I did my research well enough, I'd know what you're up to. If I knew that, I wouldn't be in this room now."

"Sure you would. We went over this. Chemistry."

"Yeah. Keep telling yourself that."

"I will. Maybe eventually you'll accept it."

"I'm surprised you aren't trying this on Lauren or Aliana." Those would be the usual suspects.

"And why would I do that when you are an option?"

"I'm not an option." I wasn't sharing the rest of my answer—that everyone went for Lauren and Aliana. It wasn't just their looks, even though they definitely had that. It was also their attitudes, their personalities, and their willingness to be completely adventurous. "What were you doing out there?" It was time to bring things back to the real issue.

"I can tell you." He rolled the cigar around in his mouth. "But it will cost you."

"Cost me?"

"Yes, cost you."

"Cost me what exactly?"

"I haven't fully decided yet, but it won't be anything you don't want to give."

"I can assure you, I don't want to give you anything but a slug in the face or a nut shot."

He laughed. "You really are a delight, Nadia."

"What were you doing out there?" I'd ask the question a million times if I had to.

"Are you ready to agree to my price?"

"How could I agree to anything if I don't know what it is?"

"Your choice, Nadia."

"Stop saying my name." I'm not sure why the name thing bothered me so much, but it did.

"No. I won't stop saying your name. You can't stop me." His smirk grew. That damn smirk. He knew he was getting to me which meant he wasn't going to stop.

"There is only one way to stop you." I wanted answers, but I was getting nowhere. "I'm leaving."

"Then we can continue this next weekend."

"I'm not coming back here." I stood up.

His eyes flashed. "I never said here."

"Then where?" I really hoped he wouldn't suggest somewhere worse. Although, I didn't know what could be worse than his room with him lying in his underwear on his bed.

"Edge of the woods. Saturday night. 9 o'clock."

"You think I'll risk getting into trouble again?" I was lucky I hadn't been caught the first time.

"You want to know what's really going on?"

"Not enough to fall for your tricks." I walked toward the door.

"Hey, Nadia."

I turned back. "What?"

"Be careful with Ryan. You don't know him as well as you think you do."

"Well, I know I don't know you at all."

"We can change that." He leaned up on an elbow. "Just let me know."

"No thanks."

He didn't say a word, but his smirk grew. I opened the door to leave, but Ryan, North, and Finn were all blocking my exit.

"Hey." I gave a small wave as I waited for them to move so I could get out of the room.

"Hey?" North sputtered out. "Is that all you have to say? What were you guys doing in there?"

"Nothing. I got nothing." I pushed him aside. "I'm going to my room."

"You okay?" Ryan was beside me in an instant. "He didn't hurt you, did he?"

"I'm fine. Don't worry."

"Nadia." Ryan followed me out to the common area in the middle of the floor. "You'd tell me the truth, right?"

"Sure. Why wouldn't I?" Admittedly, I didn't know Ryan that well, but I would have no reason to hide any of this from him.

"I can come up with a lot of reasons." There was a lot he wasn't saying, but his tone pretty much said it all.

"North would know," I noted. "Right? Since we are twins."

Ryan grinned. "I thought none of that stuff was true."

"Maybe it is. Maybe it isn't. Impossible to know, isn't it?" I smiled. "Goodnight, Ryan."

"Goodnight, Nadia."

I walked into the girls' hall and made my way down to my room. It was quiet as I unlocked my door. It was dark inside the room, but a light flicked on immediately.

"Hey, where have you been?" Jackie jumped up from her bed.

"Hey! You came." Relief and excitement in equal parts washed over me. I had been getting nervous that Jackie wasn't coming, considering she'd missed the picture and dinner. After the evening I had, I really needed her.

"Of course I did. You didn't think I would skip out on Lunar Academy, did you?" She ran over and pulled me into a hug.

"No." I hugged her back. I wasn't much of a hugger, but I made an exception with Jackie. "I didn't. But why are you so late?"

"No, the question is, why are you so late?" She brushed some of her shoulder-length hair off her shoulder, and I noticed something. Was that a tiny tattoo?

"What's that?"

"Nothing." She brushed her hair back, covering it. "So what were you doing?"

I shrugged. "I was taking care of some business."

"Business?" Jackie laughed. "You've been here, what, seven hours and you have business to attend to?"

"I'll tell you in the morning. I'm exhausted."

"Exhausted, huh?" Her eyes gleamed. "Tell me more, tell me more. Is that why Lauren came in here fit to kill you?"

"What?" I hadn't expected that.

"She wanted to know why you were going after her man."

"Her man?" I laughed.

"Ryan." Jackie sat on the edge of her bed. "I mean why in the world would she think you'd like a Grayson? And Ryan? Really?"

"I know. So it's not even worth talking about, is it?"

"Maybe, maybe not." Jackie raised an eyebrow. "You've always been a really bad liar, Nadia. And it seems some things never change."

"Tell me about your summer." I needed to change the subject.

"Oh, no, you don't. You just gave it all away. If there was nothing to talk about, you wouldn't be trying to change the subject."

"I wouldn't be? Huh?" I felt heat rise to my cheeks. Jackie could get anything out of me.

"No, you wouldn't."

"Fine. I've been hanging out with him."

"I get here a few hours late and suddenly you and Grayson are friends now?" She didn't hide her shock and possible disgust. Jackie wasn't exactly Ryan's biggest fan.

"I never said we were friends."

"Then what were you doing when you were hanging out?" She leaned back on her elbows. "If you weren't hanging out as friends."

"That's what I'll tell you about in the morning." I was way too tired and overwhelmed to discuss it before getting a few hours of sleep. If I was able to get some sleep. My mind raced with the events of the night.

"About what top secret stuff you guys were doing when you hung out?"

"Yup. Pretty much."

"You really are a weird bird, Nadia."

"And you've just discovered that now?" Her words didn't offend me in the slightest. I was fully willing to own up to my strangeness.

"No. I've known that for years, but that doesn't change that it's the truth."

"You aren't so normal yourself," I pointed out.

"I'm not normal at all, but at least I don't hang out with Ryan Grayson."

"True. That's technically true." I dug out my toiletries, pajamas, and a towel. "But I'm sure you've been doing other weird stuff." I thought of that small tattoo. It had been a tattoo, right?

When had she gotten that?

"Plenty of it. But you aren't getting a hint until you spill your beans."

"Tomorrow." I opened the door. "Tomorrow is another day." I walked out of my room and down to the communal bath. I walked into a stall and turned on the hot water. It felt amazing, but my thoughts went immediately to Ryan. That really couldn't be a good thing.

RYAN

I was up before the sunrise. That wasn't like me. Not at all. I was a night owl, not an early bird. But I wanted to talk to Nadia. I had tossed and turned all night, wondering what had been discussed. Sure, I could have called her, but I didn't know her number. That was pretty sad. I'd known the girl since we were kids, yet I'd never thought to call her. I'd have to fix that. But I'd need to see her first.

As soon as the first rays of sun showed themselves, I got up and moving. I was in the center lounge, and I wasn't going anywhere until I saw her.

"Good morning, Ryan." Lauren walked out arm in arm with Aliana.

"Hey." I feigned interest in being polite. It wasn't worth making an enemy out of her.

"How are you?"

"I'm fine." I was incredibly worried, but I didn't need to tell her that.

Finn walked out and yawned.

"It looks like you haven't slept all night."

"Geez. Thanks." I pretended to care what she thought.

"You know exactly what I mean, Ryan." She put a hand on my arm. "What's going on?"

"Nothing." I wasn't in the mood for her pretend interest. She wanted to know because she refused to be left out of anything. She couldn't care less how I actually was.

The door to the girls' hall opened again, and Nadia and her friend, Jackie, walked out together. Like everyone else, she was dressed in the Lunar Academy standard uniform of white shirt, slacks or a skirt, and a tie to match the house color—in our case blue. Unlike the others, Nadia looked super cute in hers.

"Nadia, hey." I walked right over. "Hey, Jackie. Glad you made it."

Lauren gasped. "Wait. What?"

I ignored her. "Hey, I wanted to call, but I didn't have your number."

"Oh." Nadia looked around uncomfortably.

"Can I see your phone?"

"Sure." She handed over her phone. It was in a black case with silver moons. I smiled. I liked the slight nod to what she was.

I put in my number and called it. "Okay, we're all set."

I added her as a contact in mine. At least now I'd be able to call her when I wanted.

"You okay?" Nadia headed toward the stairs.

"Sure. Are you?" She'd seemed fine the night before, but she'd been in that room with Dameon for a while. It made me nervous. Very nervous.

"Shouldn't I be?" She ran her hand over the mahogany railing on her way down.

"Okay. What did they put in the food last night?" Jackie looked between us.

"Nothing that I know of." Finn moved ahead and stopped on the landing. "Why?"

"What do you think of this?" Jackie asked Finn.

"Of what?"

"Of the fact that you are even speaking to me."

"Why wouldn't I speak to you?" Finn's brow furrowed.

"Really, Finn?" Jackie wore a textbook incredulous face. "Really?"

"What?"

Jackie smacked the side of her face with her hand. "I know you're not that oblivious. It's impossible."

"You mean because we weren't friends before. Well, it's a new place. Why shouldn't things be different?" Finn asked. "Except for your brother, Nadia. I'm still not sure about him."

Nadia shrugged. "I'm not so sure about him either, so it's okay."

I laughed. "Have you always had a sense of humor?"

"What sense of humor?" She bit back a smile.

"So... college. Huh?" Jackie stopped at the bottom of the stairs. "So much excitement."

We made our way through the lobby and outside. I assumed we were heading toward the dining hall. I knew I wanted breakfast. Some of the kids I didn't know slipped past. I wondered when we'd start to mix. My brothers never really did. They came into Lunar Academy with friends, and those are the ones they left with.

I followed Nadia over to the buffet line. She filled her plate with fruit and a couple of fruit and nut pancakes. I noticed she skipped over the sausage and bacon.

"Don't tell me you're a vegetarian," I said.

"Would it matter if I was?" She filled a mug with black coffee and set it on her tray.

"No. I'm just pointing it out."

"I'm not strictly a vegetarian, but I tend to go for the non-meat options." Nadia took a seat at the same table she'd sat at the night before. Was she one of those people? The kind that always sat in the same spot?

I sat down beside her. Jackie immediately sat on her other side. "Who's the loner?" She pointed her fork at where Dameon sat by himself.

"Don't ask." Nadia took a bite of her pancakes.

"Which means it's super important that I ask." Jackie took a strawberry from Nadia's plate.

If Nadia cared, she didn't show it. "His name is Dameon. He is annoying. Not sure what else there is to tell you."

"How about he's up to something." I figured Nadia didn't plan to keep the secret from her best friend and roommate.

North walked in, glared at us, and sat next to Dameon.

"Wait. North isn't sitting with us?" Jackie snagged another strawberry from Nadia. "Wow, times really have changed."

"That's what happens when you're late." Nadia took the strawberry back from Jackie right before she bit into it. "You miss everything."

"Who misses everything?" Finn looked up from his plate. He'd probably eaten ten strips of bacon already.

"Is this seat taken?" A girl I vaguely remembered from the night before walked over and put her hands on the back of Nadia's seat.

"Nope. Please join us." Nadia nodded toward an empty seat across from her.

She slipped into the spot next to Finn. "Great. I feel like the only one here who doesn't know anyone."

"Not the only one." Jackie pointed to Dameon in an obvious way. "I'm Jackie, and this fun bunch is Nadia, Ryan, and Finn."

"Hey, I'm Justine." The girl gave a small wave. "Nice to meet you all. Thanks for letting me sit with you."

"I saw you at the picture yesterday. Sorry, I was so distracted and didn't say anything." Nadia put her hands on the table in front of her. "That was rude."

"That's fine." Justine cut up her sausage link. "I'm just glad I don't have to look like a loner." She shot a look at Dameon and North. "Like them. Should we invite them over?"

"No," Nadia and I said at once.

"Uh, take it you aren't a fan?" Justine looked between us.

"No. Not in the slightest." Nadia returned to her pancakes. "I'm not about to pretend."

"It's a long story." I tried to soften her response. "We aren't that cold or anything."

"So you guys all know each other?" Justine set her fork down.

"Yes." Although I was beginning to realize how little I'd known Nadia. Had I been crazy?

"You went to high school together?" Justine picked up her fork again and pushed her food around on the plate.

"No. Just ran in the same circles," Nadia explained. "Kind of."

"Ryan and Finn were way too cool for us." Jackie took a long sip of her coffee. "But evidently, they aren't anymore."

"We were never too cool for them. We just had different friends." I didn't want to seem like a total jerk. But maybe I was. It didn't matter anymore anyway.

"Sure. That's what it was." Jackie leaned back in her chair. "Whatever Ryan Grayson says. He is god after all."

"Don't." Nadia glared at Jackie.

"What? You hang out with Grayson once, and now all is forgiven?"

"What is there to forgive?" I looked at Jackie. "Maybe I wasn't the friendliest to you guys before, but did I ever do anything to piss you off?"

"It's more how you move through life. You act as though you're above everything and everyone else."

"I do not." Anger surged through me.

"It kind of is." Finn shrugged. "No offense."

Jackie laughed. "Wow, Finn. I didn't expect that."

"Why not?" Finn appeared legitimately perplexed by her response. "I usually say it how it is."

"I picked an interesting table to sit at." Justine leaned an elbow on the table.

"Oh, it's about to get more interesting," Nadia mumbled.

I followed her gaze to see Dameon and North walking over. They took seats next to Justine.

"Hi, I'm Dameon." He held out his hand to her. "I don't believe we had the chance to meet yesterday."

"Hi. Justine."

"How'd you end up with this lot?" North asked. "I'm North by the way. Nadia's brother."

"They're twins," Dameon supplied.

"Twins?" Justine looked between us. "Wow. That's rar—"

Nadia cut her off. "Rare. Yes. We know."

"Sorry." Justine gave a sheepish smile. "I guess you hear that a lot?"

"All the time. It's fine." North shrugged.

"And what's your secret, Justine?" Dameon picked up a slice of bacon and took a bite.

"My secret?" Justine put a hand to her chest. "I don't have any secrets."

"Everyone has a secret. Usually way more than one. The question is, what kind it is."

"I don't have any secrets." Justine spread jam on a bagel. "But maybe the rest of you do."

"They do." Dameon leaned back in his chair.

"Is that so?" I sipped my coffee. "And I'm sure you have secrets too."

"Of course." Dameon's eyes seemed to twinkle. "I already told you; everyone has secrets."

"So what are your secrets?" Nadia pushed her food around her plate. "Since you were so eager for Justine to spill hers."

"I'll share my secrets if you show up where I asked you to last night." Dameon smiled at her.

I tried to catch Nadia's eye, but she looked away. There was no way she was going anywhere alone with Dameon. It was bad enough she'd had to go into that guy's room alone—when he was in his damn underwear.

Jackie clapped her hands. "This is almost too much. First, you're buddy-buddy with Ryan Grayson. Now, you've got secret meetings with this guy. Nadia, you little minx, you."

Nadia shot Jackie the evil eye. "Are you done?"

"Just saying it like it is. I'm sure North agrees." Jackie nodded toward North.

North frowned. "I'm more concerned with Grayson's newfound interest in my sister."

"With me?" He had to be kidding. "You're really going to sit here and say you're more worried about me than him?" I pointed at Dameon. "That's preposterous."

"Why?" Dameon turned his seat slightly so he was looking in my direction. "How am I any more dangerous than you are? In fact, she was alone with me in my room for quite some time last night and emerged unscathed."

"You were what?" Jackie's eyes widened. "Why didn't you mention those details?"

"Why do you think I didn't?" Nadia's entire body was tense. "Because of this. Who wants to sit here and listen to this?" Nadia gripped her tray.

"I'm just kidding." Jackie laughed. "You seem way higher strung than normal."

High strung? Her best friend was putting her through the meat grinder. I really didn't remember Jackie being this mean. But then again, I hadn't spent much time around her before now. "I think Nadia is behaving perfectly fine."

Nadia rewarded me with the barest hint of a smile. "I need to get ready for class."

"I'll come with you. I have Moon Phases first. What about you?" Maybe I'd get lucky and we'd have a few classes together.

Lucky? Classes together?

I really was losing it. It was because we needed to figure out who Dameon was. Nope. That was bullshit, and I knew it.

"I'm in that class as well." Nadia stood up and grabbed her tray.

I did the same. "See you guys later." I ignored the look I was getting from Finn. I needed to talk to Nadia, and I planned to do it any way I could.

"You okay?" I waited until we were outside the dining hall to ask her. Wolves had good hearing.

"Yeah. Why wouldn't I be?" She pushed her hands into the front pockets of her skirt.

"Because your best friend is a bitch." Might as well call it what it was.

"Wow." Her eyes roamed my face, as if searching for a joke. "That's pretty harsh."

"Really?" I thought my assessment was a good one. "You're disagreeing?"

"She's not usually like that."

"So, it's not just my hazy memory. Something is off." From what I could tell, something major was off with Jackie, but maybe she just had a crappy summer.

"Maybe." Nadia shrugged. "Or maybe I'm more sensitive. I don't know."

"This has nothing to do with being sensitive. Don't even go there." I didn't know why it was so damn important to me that she not shrug this off. I guess I felt protective of her. Which was insane. Why was I feeling protective of Nadia Hazel?

"Okay..." Nadia seemed just as confused by my behavior as I was.

"So, what was that about meeting Dameon again?" We needed to make a plan. I wanted to be pissed I hadn't heard about this from her, but I'd barely seen her that morning.

"He claims he has something to show me."

"I got that much from the conversation, but when and where? And you know you aren't doing it yourself."

Her eyes narrowed. "Oh, I'm not, am I? Because you can tell me what to do now?"

Yes, yes, I could. Because I couldn't sit back and let her do something stupid. But that wasn't the kind of thing she wanted to hear. "I'm just trying to make sure you don't wind up dead. That okay with you?"

"How about I worry about keeping myself alive, and you worry about how to make sure I don't get caught shifting again when I go."

"Oh, is that it? You'll use my help for something like that, but I'm not supposed to worry about you?"

"Why do you care what happens to me anyway?" Nadia stopped a few feet from the door to the dorms. "I mean I get you wanting answers last night. I get you not wanting me to get caught so I can't squeal on you. But apart from all that, why do you care in the slightest?"

"Like I should know?" I had no idea how to answer her. I wished I did. "But does it really matter? I don't want you dying. Is that a bad thing?"

"It's not a bad thing, but it's an unnecessary thing." She slipped a finger through a belt loop on her skirt.

"It's unnecessary that you don't die?" I didn't let my thoughts go to how much I wanted to slip my hand underneath her skirt. "That's a bit harsh."

"You know what I mean. I can take care of myself."

"And I don't doubt that—most of the time—but we don't know who Dameon really is, or what he wants."

"Do we ever really know who anyone is, or what they want?" She eyed a group of girls walking toward us. She stepped off to the side to give them space to pass.

"No." I waited until the girls disappeared inside to answer. "No, we don't. But there are some people we can trust."

"Until you can't." There was a hollowness to her voice, a sadness I wished I could make disappear.

"Are you talking about Jackie or North?" I assumed she meant them. "Or both?"

"I'm not talking about anyone or anything in particular. I'm just talking. We should go get ready for class."

"We don't want to be late for Moon Phases." I grinned. "Very serious material."

She smiled. "It might be interesting."

"Even though I am positive you already know everything the professor is going to teach." Maybe I hadn't taken the time to really get to know Nadia before, but I did know she was smart. Seriously smart.

"Not true."

"Oh?" I raised an eyebrow. "Is there a single thing about the phases of the moon that you don't already know?"

"It's impossible to know everything there is to know about a topic." She crossed her arms over her chest.

"But you can know a lot."

"And you know a lot about moon phases too." She gave me a knowing look. "So, don't pretend otherwise."

"Am I pretending?"

"You tend to pretend a lot. It's like you don't want people to know you're smart." Her gaze was pointed.

"For a girl that's never gone to school with me, you're inferring a lot."

"Am I wrong?"

"Maybe. Maybe not. You're just going to have to wait and see."

"I'm not falling for that."

"Falling for what?"

"The teasing." She headed toward the door. "I couldn't care less about it. I'm not into you."

"You are into me. I smelled your—"

She stopped short and spun back to look at me. "Yes, I got turned on by a naked man. Is that all that shocking for an eighteen-year-old girl? We all know you're quite the physical specimen. It was only natural for me to feel that way, but does that mean I am into you? No. I had the exact same reaction to seeing Dameon in his underwear."

My wolf growled. "But nothing happened."

"Would it matter if it did? You don't seem to understand that what I do, say, or feel is none of your business."

"We're in this together now, so it's most definitely my business." It went far beyond figuring out who Dameon was, but I wasn't admitting that.

"How can we be in anything together if we don't know what it is?" she shot back.

"Because we know it's something, and that's all that matters."

"That doesn't make logical sense."

"Not everything is logical." I walked past her. "Come on. Aren't you the one worried we'll be late for class?"

NADIA

I waited at the edge of the woods, silently cursing myself for getting involved in this stupidity in the first place. What was the point? If North wanted to get himself into a mess, that was his right. Just because I was his sister, it didn't mean it was my job to keep him out of trouble. Just like it wasn't his job to worry about what boys I got involved with. Not that I planned to get involved with any boys. Especially not Ryan Grayson. I certainly didn't want to go there. He ate girls like me for breakfast. It didn't take going to school with him to know his reputation—or that of his brothers. They were all notorious playboys, and Ryan was no exception.

It was not that I hated Ryan; it was more that we existed on different planes. Neither better nor worse than the other, but certainly not meant to orbit the same path.

But this was no time to think about Ryan. This was the time to stay focused and figure out exactly what Dameon was doing.

Yet, I couldn't shake my worry about North. It's not that we'd been close for years, but at least when we lived at home we'd talked. We barely communicated now. I'd gone back and forth all week over whether to go or not. I'd been so focused on the decision I'd barely listened to my lectures. Ultimately I'd known I had to show up.

It was still hot out even though it was after nine. That was typical of early September in the deep south. Yet I still wished there was some sort of breeze. I was hot in my t-shirt and shorts. I'd long since changed out of my uniform, but I didn't want to shift too early. For all I knew, Dameon was trying to get me in trouble. So instead, I waited. I knew Ryan was watching from somewhere. I'd convinced him to keep his distance, but that didn't mean he wasn't close. He probably hadn't listened to me. I'd seen the reservation in his eyes. I tried not to let it bother me that his eyes were locked on me somehow, watching. That was nothing compared to everything else.

Footsteps sounded, and I tensed. A familiar scent floated to my nose. My muscles loosened as North walked toward me. I flashed him a look. "What? You knew I wasn't letting you go alone."

He was right, but I thought he'd try to hide it better. It wasn't his style to come right out and show me where he was. Usually, he'd drive me insane by making me find him.

"What happened to trusting Dameon?" I asked.

"I do trust him, in theory. That doesn't mean I want you running alone with him."

I didn't want to admit it, but I was glad North was here. I didn't trust Dameon either. "Okay."

"You could say thank you." North rolled up the cuffs of his shirt. He hadn't changed out of his uniform. That wasn't surprising either. North liked to keep things formal. The uniform was probably his favorite part of Lunar Academy.

"And why would I say that?"

"Because you didn't want to do this alone, and you knew you couldn't bring Ryan. I'm surprised you didn't bring Jackie though."

"I haven't seen her since lunch." I thought for a brief moment at how odd that was. Granted, we didn't have any classes together, but I still hadn't even seen her in passing. That had largely been how things had worked for us since the semester started. I hoped that would eventually change.

"What happened to her this summer?" North once again made me think of a conversation with Ryan. Were the two more alike than I thought, or was my life really that narrowly focused?

"What do you mean?" Did North know something I didn't, or was he fishing for information? My brother wasn't the type to bring stuff up unless it was for a reason. He didn't like wasting words.

"Come on. Something is up. She's even more of a bitch than normal."

"She's usually not a bitch." Okay. This was essentially the same conversation I'd had with Ryan. I already knew something was off with her, but then again, she thought something was off with me since I was spending my time with Ryan and Dameon.

"Yet, she is right now. See? Even you admit it."

"She's been bitchy." Thankfully that first breakfast was the worst of it though when she'd Implied I was sleeping around. I couldn't even rationalize that one away. "I readily admit to that."

"Something is up, and you've known Jackie forever. Shouldn't this concern you more?"

"Since when do you care about Jackie? It's not like she's your friend." I wouldn't have used the term enemies to describe them, but there was definitely a heavy dose of friction between them. It was probably normal. Most people didn't love their sibling's best friends.

"But she's your friend, which means I have a vested interest in making sure she doesn't go off the deep end and take you with her."

"I won't go off the deep end." I had my flaws—we all did—but my mental health was strong.

"Yet, you're hanging out with Ryan Grayson."

"So? And Jackie has nothing to do with that." Not to mention that Ryan wasn't dangerous or any part of the issue at hand. "Quit trying to pull Ryan into everything." Yes, a few days before, I wouldn't have believed I'd be spending time with him, but that didn't mean it was a bad thing.

"You have to admit it's weird." North glanced around us. "Really weird."

"Why?" I lifted my long hair off my back to cool off.

"Why is it weird that I'm spending a little bit of time with Ryan?"

"A little bit of time?" He raised an eyebrow. "Who have you spent the most time with since you arrived?"

"No one in particular. We've been here less than a month," I pointed out. It's not like I'd been shacking up with him for years. "Where is Dameon? He better show up."

"He'll show up."

"How are you so sure?" North was rarely sure about things when they involved other people. He never doubted himself though.

"Because I am."

"Oh, really good explanation."

"He wants you to see this. I'd rather keep you out of it. To protect you. But we need your brain." His forehead furrowed. He was nervous. I didn't like that he was nervous. But, there was something else about his words that jumped out more.

"Wait." I felt a small smile spread across my face. "You're admitting to needing me for something?" This was a first. I didn't think he had the ability to admit something like that. He hadn't asked me for help since the second grade, even though there were plenty of times where my help could have been rather useful. Lucky for him, I had no problem offering him help regardless if he asked. Hence why I was in the woods, waiting for Dameon.

"Yes. This isn't what you're expecting. I can tell you that."

"Then tell me."

"It would be much easier to show you." He rubbed the back of his neck.

"Then show me." I was tired of waiting.

North shook his head. "We need Dameon."

"Why?"

"Because he knows how to find what we need to find."

I put my hands in my back pockets. "Well, he better get here fast. I really don't want to get caught." The first night had been enough of a close call.

"Ryan likes you. He won't let you get expelled." North turned his head slightly, and I knew he was stretching his hearing. I knew each and every one of his mannerisms.

"He doesn't like me, and that doesn't matter. Even if he did, he can't save me from trouble if it's coming. And you know Mom and Dad won't."

"Nope. They'll make you face the consequences yourself." North said exactly what I already knew. "Just like they'd make me. But that's not a bad thing. We have good parents, remember?"

"I'm not interested in debating the successes or failures of our parents. Yes, they have the right ideals. Do they make their share of mistakes too? Yes. But that's part of life." There was beauty in the imperfect, as cliché as that sounded.

"Are you two done yammering about your parents?" Dameon sauntered over.

"Why are you late?" Lateness was one of those

things I couldn't stand. It was one thing when you were late for yourself, but to be late when you specifically asked someone to meet you was an entirely different thing.

"I had a few matters to deal with." He stopped with that small and incomplete explanation.

"Matters, huh?" I didn't bother to hide my annoyance. "And you couldn't call?"

"First, I don't have your number. Second, did you really bring your phone?"

I rolled my eyes. My irritation toward him reached an all new level. Why was he always so damn smug? He was right, of course, but that didn't mean I wanted to admit it.

"You done giving me a hard time about being a tad bit late?" he asked.

"It is more than a tad bit late. It's thirty minutes."

"That's still less than an hour. That makes it a tad." Dameon was so relaxed. So nonchalant. It was so the opposite of how I felt that it drove me nuts.

"You have a funny system of measuring time." I was holding in my annoyance.

"It works for me."

"Okay. Let's stop wasting more of it." North ran a hand through his hair. "I'm going with you guys."

"Of course." Dameon nodded. "I assumed as much. Why else would you be here?"

"See? He isn't looking to hurt you." North gave me a satisfied smile. "Like I told you."

"Should we shift?" I asked, ignoring North.

"Yes." Dameon pulled off his t-shirt. For the second

time in two days, I saw him shirtless. I hated to admit it, but he didn't look all that bad.

"Be right back." I walked back behind a tree to change.

"Really?" Dameon laughed. "You're afraid to undress in front of me?"

"I don't want to undress in front of North either." Ugh. That sounded awful.

Dameon lifted a brow. "But he's your brother..."

"Exactly." I don't want to undress in front of him. Wolves or not.

"Has she always been like this?" Dameon asked North.

"I don't exactly love getting naked in front of her either." North had his shirt off, but I could tell he was waiting to take his pants off until I turned around.

"You both are odd." Dameon took off his pants.

"Okay. I don't really care." I looked away as soon as I got an eyeful. I made sure the trees blocked me enough before I stripped down, stashed my clothes, and reached for my wolf. She immediately took over.

Dameon and North waited for me a little farther in. Without any warning, Dameon took off into the woods.

He ran fast, and unlike Ryan, he wasn't slowing pace to stay close to me. North hung back and circled around me. He knew it annoyed me when he did it, but I also knew it was his way of making sure I didn't get left behind.

I pushed myself harder. While I might not be able to catch up with Dameon, I could at least get close.

North ran circles around me, encouraging me forward. It instantly brought me back to childhood. The circling had been a frequent game we played when we were still getting used to our wolves. For a moment, I was nearly able to forget that we were hours from home and running who the heck knew where, breaking multiple rules in the process. Yet I was doing all of this by choice. As much as North complained about us being at the academy, our parents wouldn't have ever forced us to go. It had always been our choice. But giving up the opportunity to train with the finest teachers wasn't a real choice for me.

But, then Dameon disappeared. Or it looked like he did. We were nearing the spot where I'd lost them earlier. I felt the thick mist before I saw it. Despite every part of my body warring with me to turn around, I ran straight into the fog. It was so thick I could barely see, but I pushed on. My body tingled with alarm, and it was that alarm that kept me from stopping to examine the haze. There had to be magic at play here. There was no other possibility. It was thick, yet like no natural mist I'd ever witnessed before.

Soon enough, I was out of the haze. Now we were in a darker and lusher section of forest. I wanted to look behind me, but I didn't want to risk losing the others. Thankfully, Dameon stopped. I looked back. I could see the barest hint of the haze—of the magic.

Dameon nipped at me.

I growled out of instinct. He nipped again, and I realized he was trying to get my attention. He bowed his head and nodded it in a westward direction.

I glanced that way but didn't see much. I could sense something though. Other wolves. We were too far out for me to determine who they were, but my instincts told me there was a pack.

Dameon ran faster, and once again, North held back near me instead. He was so close to me this time I was tempted to growl at him to make sure he stayed out of my space.

But his eyes warned me from doing anything.

And a moment later, I understood. On the other side of a thick grouping of trees in a clearing there was a circle of wolves. It took me a moment to realize they weren't why North was so close—the girl standing in their center was.

Jackie?

My heart rate accelerated as I zeroed in on her. Before I could comprehend my best friend was off with a group of strangers deep in the woods, hidden by magic, in the middle of the night, a guy I didn't recognize spoke.

"Welcome back," his deep voice began. He was tall and lanky, much thinner than most male wolves I'd come across. His stature was similar to mine instead. "Thank you for returning for another meeting. I am hoping we're able to get through more tonight than our previous meeting as we have everyone here this time. He pointed to Jackie. "Don't think that you won't have to pay a price for missing the last meeting. You knew the terms of membership."

"Yes, sir." Jackie bowed her head before bowing.

I tried to swallow a gasp. Wolves did not bow before others. It wasn't in our nature.

"I assure you I had a good reason," Jackie said.

"And will you share this reason with the group?" His voice was angry, doing nothing to hide a snide edge.

"Yes." Jackie looked down. "I had to terminate an enemy."

Terminate? I repeated the word in my head. There was only one meaning of the word terminate I could think of, and it wasn't a good thing. But there was no way she would have done something like that. Not Jackie. There had to be a different explanation. A different meaning.

"And the termination was successful?" The leader's voice lilted with something akin to excitement. Who the hell was this guy? And why were they terminating anyone?

None of this made sense.

"It was, sir. A clean job. No one will suspect a thing when they find the body."

No. I wasn't wrong about her use of the word. My stomach churned, and I worried I might lose everything I'd eaten at breakfast.

"Good." The man patted her head as if she were a dog or a small child. There was nothing so insulting to a wolf. "Good, girl."

I looked at North. Was he seeing this? He shook his head. This was officially beyond weird.

"Again, I'm sorry for missing the meeting. I should

have reported in earlier." She was still avoiding eye contact with the man as if she were ashamed. "I know there may be punishment."

"Yes, but the punishment will be mitigated for doing what you had to do for our kind, even if it meant shedding human blood."

Human blood? Every inch of me froze. I hurt. My stomach turned more, and I knew I would struggle to keep anything down. "Yes, sir."

"You may return to your feet." He raised his hand as if commanding her to stand.

"Thank you, sir." Jackie lifted her head so she was now looking directly at him.

"Are there any other admissions that must be made?" the man asked.

There was only silence.

"Very well." The man stepped into the middle of the circle. "We may turn our attention to our main business. Arnold, where are we on recruitment?"

"We have several good possibilities." A bald man with a large scar across his right cheek spoke.

"How are we with Grayson?" the leader asked.

Grayson? Did they mean Ryan? None of his brothers were at the academy now, so they had to mean him, right?

"I have a new in with him now." Jackie bowed slightly. "He has taken an interest in my roommate. I will offer my help to leverage some time with him."

"And you believe he will trust you?" a girl with two long blond braids asked. "I thought the two of you weren't close friends."

"Our families go way back. And I can tell his interest in my roommate is strong. I can take care of it."

"Your roommate is Ms. Hazel," the leader said as a statement. "We could use her too."

Jackie laughed. "Nadia? Are you kidding? Do you know who her parents are?"

"Yes. But I also know who your parents are, and you have been nothing but helpful to our cause."

"My parents are abominations. I have no allegiance to them. Nadia has allegiance to hers."

"And her brother?" the leader asked. "Is he as loyal to their ways?"

"Even more so."

What? Why would she think that? North had more of a strained relationship with my parents than I did. Jackie knew that. Was she purposely lying?

"Still, see what you can do. A set of twins would be helpful to our cause." The leader rubbed his chin. "Perhaps Grayson will help. Is Ms. Hazel as interested in him as he is in her?"

"Oh, absolutely." Jackie grinned wickedly. "I've never seen her this aroused by a guy before."

Aroused? Seriously? Jackie really was a bitch. Not that talking about me this way was the worst thing she'd ever done. Terminating someone was way worse.

"Then find a way. If you can get Grayson and the twins, you will be handsomely rewarded."

"I'll deliver all three."

She was out of her mind. I wasn't entirely sure what their cause was, but if they killed humans, there was no way North and I were joining. Or *Ryan*. Somehow, I knew he wouldn't be down for this either.

The Graysons were a powerful and public family, but their politics were in line with the mainstream. They believed wolves were superior, but I'd never heard them push for hurting humans.

"And what happens if she can't?" the blond girl asked. "Because we're putting too much in her hands. I'll gladly help out as needed. Perhaps I can work on the boy twin."

North huffed. I felt a laugh build inside my wolf. That girl had no idea what she was up against. North was as picky as they came when it came to girls.

"I can handle them all." Jackie nodded her head. "I have relationships with them already in place. I grew up with the twins. They trust me. If anyone can convince them to join, it's me."

"Even North?" the girl asked. "That is his name?"

"Yes. Even North. He's had a crush on me for years."

North made a coughing sound. Dameon chomped at him.

"Did you hear that?" Arnold glanced around.

Dameon nipped at me. I knew that was his way of telling me we needed to go. I wanted to listen more to what they were discussing, but my gut told me to leave. Getting caught wouldn't help at all.

RYAN

I was getting impatient. They'd been gone too long. I needed to find them. Well, I needed to find Nadia. Sure, I was interested in what the hell was going on, but I was also interested in her. Far too interested in her.

A rustling noise found its way to my ears, and then came her scent. Fuck, I loved the way she smelled. Why was her scent so impossible to resist? It had me wanting her. Needing her.

Before I could get too bent out of shape, I smelled the others. Trying to get with Nadia wouldn't earn me any favors with North.

I waited a few minutes, hoping they'd find me so we could get back to the dorms. Technically, we could be out at night, but I really didn't feel like getting questioned by Professor Blair again.

"Ryan, hey." Nadia ran over. She tugged down on her

tank top—a sign she'd just shifted back. How did I know that already? How did I know so much about this girl?

"You okay?" I looked her over. Other than a tank strap partially slipping off her shoulder in a ridiculously enticing way, she looked like she always did.

"Yes, I'm fine." She turned to Dameon and North, who were a few feet behind her. "What the hell was that?"

That was a good question. One I wanted to know the answer to. Fast.

"Those were the Elites. Well, and some new blood." Dameon rubbed his hands together.

"You mean Jackie?" Nadia's eyes fell. "That's the new blood?"

"Some of it." Dameon pulled on a t-shirt. "There's some other new blood there too."

"I'm sorry you had to see that, Nadia." North patted her back. "And hear it."

Wait what? "Okay. Someone needs to fill me in. Now."

"It was awful." Nadia looked up at me. "Awful, Ryan. Jackie—she's. It's horrible."

"I told you something was up with her." North shifted his weight from foot to foot.

"Wait. You knew, didn't you?" Nadia's eyes widened on her brother. "That's why you were so close to me."

North's face softened when he met Nadia's gaze. "I heard them talk about her last time... but you know. Seeing and hearing is entirely different."

"Well, now we know why she was late the first night." Nadia sighed.

"You may know, but I sure as hell don't." Heat burned through my core. "Someone want to fill me in?"

"We will." Dameon tied his boots. "Soon."

"Considering they mentioned him by name." North gave me a sidelong glance. "I suppose we have no choice."

"What? Who mentioned me?" The heat in my core spread. I wasn't used to being kept in the dark about anything.

"Well, they said Grayson... technically, it could have been one of his brothers, but he's the only one here." Nadia looked away, as if trying to avoid my eyes.

That annoyed me more than it probably should have. "Okay. Someone needs to talk. Now." It was bad enough that I didn't know what was going on, but now I'd come to find out someone was talking about me?

"Did Jackie ever tell you why she was late, Nadia?" North asked, ignoring me completely.

Nadia shook her head. "No. Which is strange, but I guess it's not strange now. Although, she seems to think she can pull all three of us into this. Which is absolutely ridiculous."

"Hello? Can we focus here, guys? What is going on? You can't tell me people are talking about me and not give me more to go on."

"Not here." Dameon took a seat on the back of a metal bench. "But I appreciate how persistent you are. Are you this way about everything?"

"And we can talk more about Jackie too," North added. "I'm sure it all ties in."

"What is your fixation on Jackie?" Nadia crossed her arms. "Was she right? Do you like her?"

"Of course not!" North's face turned bright red. "How can you even say that?"

"We can deal with all of this later." Dameon stood up. "But we need to go."

We started back for the dorms. I felt like I had to say something to Dameon before he changed his mind and made this harder than it needed to be. "Thanks for not fighting about telling me."

"I always planned to involve you, but I knew I needed to show the twins first. Things have to be done in a certain order or they don't work."

I had no idea what he was talking about, but I'd resist making some snide remark. "Okay."

"You do have will power." Dameon grinned.

Nadia glanced over. "What do you mean?"

"He wants to say something to me, but he won't. He gets that it isn't in his interest. This one isn't as dumb as he looks." He laughed. He was trying to bait me. I wouldn't take it.

We reached the dorms. "Should we use the soundproof room again?" I asked.

"Soundproof room?" North raised an eyebrow.

Nadia gave me a look.

I shrugged. "Oh, sorry." I'd assumed that we were all working together now, so it didn't hurt to tell them. Maybe I'd assumed wrong.

"Don't be." Her expression softened. "I was about to suggest it anyway. I'm just giving you a hard time."

This seemed to be the night of people giving me a hard time. Yet it was oddly not an issue when it was Nadia. I kind of liked it.

I'd officially lost it.

"So you've seen the soundproof room, huh?" Dameon led us back behind the stairs. He ran his hand over the wall and found the secret door—like Nadia had.

"I guess you aren't the only one who does research." I gently nudged Nadia's shoulder with my own.

"No. I always do my research. It's something you should probably start doing too." Dameon frowned.

"You're probably right." Maybe I wouldn't be relying on other people to fill me in if I did.

Dameon grinned. "I still find it interesting Nadia took Ryan down here." He started down the stairs. The rest of us followed. "Very Interesting. Was it to be alone?"

"No, it was to talk." Nadia grunted. "Finn was with us."

"Like bringing him along makes it any better?" North grumbled. "What the hell has gotten into you, Nadia?"

"Nothing." She bristled. "Stop doubting me."

"How can I do anything but doubt you if you do stupid things like that?" North stomped down the stairs.

"Ugh. Stop!" She wrung her hands. "Stop, stop, stop!"

"All we did was talk, like she said. Stop thinking less of your sister." I scowled at North, burning a hole into the back of his head with my eyes.

"I realize she wouldn't be stupid enough to do something with you, but that doesn't mean it wasn't stupid to bring you guys down here alone. Stupid and dangerous."

"Get over this obsession you have of me hurting her. I won't." I'd never hurt her. Not that I'd hurt any other girl. I understood the concept of consent and respect.

"I have no reason to trust you." North reached the bottom of the stairs and pivoted to glare at me.

"You have no reason not to trust me either." This was ridiculous. I shouldn't have to make my case every time I was around this guy.

"All right. You two don't like each other." Dameon held up his hands. "I get it. I get it loud and clear. Nothing we can do about that now, but there are other things we can deal with."

"Agree to disagree for now?" I held out a hand to North. Generally, I wouldn't have given in like that, but I wanted to know how to hell I tied into whatever was going on in the woods.

"Sure." North accepted my hand. "For now."

"Good." Dameon smiled. "Aren't you glad that's out of the way?" He looked at Nadia. "I don't know about you, but I get tired of the alpha bullshit."

Nadia laughed. "Oh, yeah? Right."

"What?" Dameon stepped backward until he was close to the stone wall of the room at the back.

"Like you don't do the same alpha bullshit?" Nadia rolled her eyes. "If anything, you're worse."

"Worse than Grayson?" North laughed dryly. "No one is worse than him."

"I do have a first name." Normally, I didn't care. Tons of people called me Grayson, but I was already pissed off at North.

"Didn't you two just agree to stop this pissing contest?" Nadia frowned. "Come on. Keep it together."

"Yes." North let out a slow deep breath. "We did. But Grayson here—"

"Ryan," I interrupted.

"When have you ever cared what I call you?" North pointed at me.

"He doesn't." Nadia sat down on the third from the bottom step. "He's just giving you a hard time. Just like you're giving him a hard time by calling him Grayson. So how about we stop worrying about names? We don't need names."

She was right, of course. "What was going on out there?" I asked.

"Dameon, why don't you explain since you seem to know all about it?" Nadia yawned. She looked exhausted. "After all, you were the one who wanted us to see it."

"Absolutely." Dameon walked away from the wall over to where North and I stood. "But first, I need to know that you three will help destroy them."

"You want us to agree to destroy a group we know nothing about?" He couldn't be serious.

"Well, they are okay with killing humans..." Nadia trailed off.

"What the hell?" Where did that left turn come from.?

"Jackie killed a human." Nadia visibly shook. "She

called it a termination, but I'm pretty sure she killed someone. My roommate killed someone."

"You're switching rooms." North walked over and sat beside her. "But I am sure you knew that already."

"She can't." Dameon shook his head.

"What?" Was he crazy? Also, it wasn't his decision. "You want her to sleep in the same room with a murderer?"

"Jackie won't hurt her. You heard what went down, Nadia. They want you. She can't kill you. Plus, you're a Wolf Born. Your bloodline is pure. That means something to them."

"Okay. Start talking." Knowing I was involved was one thing. Knowing Nadia was sleeping in the same room as a murderer crossed the line. "Obviously, we don't support the killing of innocent humans."

"Obviously?" Dameon laughed dryly. "I'm not so sure it's obvious."

"Why would we want to kill humans? What am I missing here?" Sure, humans were far weaker than we were, but that didn't mean I wanted them dead.

"Just explain things to us." Nadia put her hands in her lap. "You know we're not joining them."

"None of us know anything for sure." Dameon walked to one of the exterior walls and ran his hand over it as he had done upstairs. He pressed his palm into it; there was a small groaning sound and a bookshelf appeared. "You never know what's hiding right under the surface."

First a secret room and now a secret bookshelf? What other secrets did the Wolf Born dormitory hold?

"Yeah, I do." Nadia moved to stand. "I'll never support anyone hurting an innocent. That's preposterous. I love humans. My family loves humans. That's why we'll never be fully accepted."

"That's not true." It bothered me to hear her say that. "You are accepted." They were—mostly—but there was no secret that there were some of our kind who didn't like those of us who closely aligned with humans. Still, that didn't mean they weren't welcome. If anything, it was a lack of financial resources that set the Hazels apart—as Lauren had so callously pointed out on move-in day.

"Yes, it is." Nadia sighed. "Please don't lie. I was starting to tolerate you, and if you start lying, that will change."

"Fine. Do some of our kind look down on your family? Yes. That's as far as I'll go in terms of agreeing with you."

"At least it's not a lie," Nadia mumbled.

"Okay. Just explain everything." North gritted his teeth. "They need to know."

"Wait." Nadia leaned back against the railing, her eyes glued to North. She was exhausted, and I understood why. I felt the same way. "You already know?"

"I know some. Not all."

"Just explain." I was done asking. If I didn't get answers, heads would roll. "I know North finding out first might annoy you, Nadia, but this is getting old."

"Fine," Dameon insisted. "Nadia and North came with me to see a meeting of a group called the Elites."

"The Elites?" Was I hearing this right? "There's a group of wolves out there called the Elites?"

"What you want to say is how the hell aren't you apart of it?" Dameon's eyes gleamed. "And why weren't you told of them until now?"

It irked me the way he seemed to always know what I was thinking. I'd never admit to it though.

"Continue." I folded my arms over my chest, eyeing him.

Dameon smirked. "Very well. These Elites are hell bent on bringing the wolves out into the public eye no matter the cost to humans. Even if it brings a war that leads to the death of millions."

"The death of millions?" I wasn't surprised by his words, considering what I'd heard about Jackie, but it still made no sense to me. "Why? I mean, I understand wanting get out of the shadows, but why risk hurting innocents?"

"Some want to enslave them if they don't cooperate. Is that much better?" North clasped his hands together. When his hands made contact, the sound echoed in the small room.

Nadia shivered. I wanted to put an arm around her, but I wasn't sure if that would upset her more. Also, I knew the action would set North off again. Since that wasn't top on my list, I refrained.

"No. it's not better. Although, I suppose anything is better than death," I said. Death was so final.

"Not everything is better than death." Nadia's eyes had clouded over when I shifted my attention back to her. "I'd rather die than become a slave. To lose the ability to have free will." Another shiver slipped through her.

"Same here." North nodded. "I couldn't live that way."

"The whole idea is that you don't have a choice." Dameon pulled a book from the bookcase and flipped through it. "You have to live that way regardless of what you want."

"At least you'd have a shot—at freedom, and a second chance at life." Death was the end. After that, there was nothing. They couldn't really mean they'd take that option.

"Wow." Nadia put a hand to her throat. "I wouldn't have pegged you to be that type."

"What type?"

"A romantic."

I shifted on my feet. "I'm not a romantic."

"Not in terms of relationships," she explained. "But in the way you view the world. What you just said is something a romantic would say."

"Okay. This is a great whole psychoanalysis and all, but let's keep moving." North joined Dameon at the bookcase. He looked at whatever book he held, but didn't seem particularly interested in whatever was on its pages.

"This isn't psychoanalysis. You know that, North." Nadia sighed. "Don't play dumb."

"Regardless, we can't let the Elites continue to build

its numbers." Dameon slammed the book closed, setting off a plume of dust. "We need to infiltrate them."

"And that's where Ryan comes in, right?" North's voice was barely a whisper. "I knew there was a reason you wanted to deal him in."

"Excuse me?"

"You're their number one target for recruitment." Dameon returned the book to the shelf and pulled out another.

"Why me?"

"Why not you?" He held out the book.

I accepted it. It was a book on the history of pack politics.

"You're a Grayson." North perused the shelf. "Need I say more?"

"I'm not the only student here from a well-known family."

"Your family is more than well-known." Nadia was looking right at me. "And you know it."

"Still, I don't believe they'd go through much effort to recruit me." Being from a well-known family meant I tried to stay under the radar and out of trouble.

"Should I tell him what Jackie said, or do you guys want to?" Nadia asked.

"You can." Dameon gestured for her to continue.

I prepared myself. I had a strong feeling I wouldn't like what I was about to hear.

"She thinks she can use your supposed interest in me to help recruit you."

"My supposed interest in you?"

"Yes. I know how ridiculous that is."

"What's ridiculous? Me being into you, or her using it to recruit me?"

"Both."

"Well, the first part isn't ridiculous. The second part is." Did Nadia really think it was that hard to believe I wanted her? Had she looked at herself recently? Didn't she realize how gorgeous she was? How perfect her breasts looked in that tank top? How her smile alone was enough to turn me on?

"It's all ridiculous." Nadia redid her ponytail. The edge of her tank top slipped up when she lifted her arms, revealing a trace of skin that did things to me. "But either way, that's her plan."

"My vote is that you let her think it's working." Dameon pressed his palm next to the bookcase. There was a groan, and then the shelf disappeared.

I held out the book to him, but he shook his head.

I shrugged. I guessed I was keeping it for the time being. "Wait. You really want me to pretend to be part of this Elite group?"

"Yes." Dameon rubbed his hands together. "It's our ticket to inside information."

"What about us?" North gestured between himself and Nadia. "Do we play along too?"

"I take it they want to recruit you guys as well?" I asked. Dameon had alluded to that earlier when discussing why it was safe for Nadia to continue living with Jackie.

"Yes." Nadia pulled the hair tie out of her hair,

evidently giving up on the ponytail. The result was that her long curly hair now hung down her back. She looked so good with her hair down. "They don't think they can, but Jackie seems to think she can turn us. It's weird, and it makes me super nervous."

"This whole thing should make you nervous," Dameon pointed out. "If it didn't, I'd worry."

"I need more information." That was the bottom line. I wasn't agreeing to anything until I knew more. "You can't expect me to take this all at face value. I haven't even seen these wolves. Who are they anyway? I mean, would I know any of them?"

"You think I'm lying to you?" There was something akin to hurt in Nadia's voice. "I don't know most of them, but that doesn't mean it didn't happen."

"No." I didn't hesitate. "But how do you know what you saw was what you thought it was?"

She seemed to think over my words. "I don't. Except I saw and heard Jackie. I know I didn't imagine that."

"I know, but how do we know Dameon isn't playing games with us?" Because for me, that was what this all came down to.

"You don't." Dameon started toward the stairs.

"Then why should we agree to your plan?" Was he really admitting that so easily?

"Because if it's all a game, what does it hurt to play along?"

"What does it hurt? We might get caught in a trap. We might get framed for something I want no part in." And those were only the tip of the iceberg. If my mom would be pissed about my facial hair in the picture, I didn't want to think about what she'd do to me if I was part of a scandal this size.

"So be careful." Dameon started up the stairs. "If you're as powerful as everyone seems to think, that shouldn't be a challenge."

"I need to do my own research." That was the only way I would even consider going along with this plan.

"Go ahead." Dameon stopped at the top of the stairs. "You won't find anything. The Elites aren't stupid."

"Nadia can find something. She's the ultimate researcher."

"Thanks for the confidence." She put a hand on my arm. The contact sent a wave of awareness through me. "But I'm not promising anything."

"Promise to try." Otherwise, we had to tell someone. We couldn't play this game, but clearly, we also couldn't let it go. "I'm not agreeing to anything unless you do."

Nadia looked me straight in the eyes. "You have to help."

"That works for me." I couldn't let her do this without me. I'd worry about her too damn much. Plus, this was a reason to spend more time with her.

"Deal." Nadia held out her hand. "Come on. I know you like to shake on things."

I accepted the handshake. "Deal."

NADIA

"*H*ey, Nadia. You up?" Jackie asked as the door cracked open. I'd been back for hours, but I most definitely had not gotten any sleep.

"Hey, kind of." I tried to sound tired, but really, I was nervous, angry, and stressed.

"Can we talk a little bit?" She was changed already somehow. There was no sign of the dirt that had been all over her when I saw her in the woods.

"Sure. Everything okay?" I wondered where she'd cleaned herself up. Her shower stuff was still in our room.

"Yeah. Things are good." She sat down on the edge of my bed.

I searched her face in the low light coming from the lamp on her side of the room. I'd left that on for her, so she wouldn't blind me with the overhead light. "What's up?"

"We need to catch up. I have no clue what's going on with you."

"I can say the same thing about you." Or rather I knew what was up with her. Well, some of it.

"Not much for me to share. My life is boring; you know that." Her eyes twinkled when she said that. Was that her tell when she lied? Or was she having fun messing with me?

"That's not true."

"Sure it is. What exciting things have ever happened to me?" She put a hand to her chest. "But you. Exciting things always happen to you."

I sat up, bolstering my pillows to make it easier. "Not true. My life is not exciting."

"Ryan Grayson?" She patted my legs through the blanket. "That isn't exciting?"

"Him as a wolf? As a person? I'm not following how that makes anything exciting for me."

"Oh?" She laughed. "You still pretending there's nothing going on there?" She was really doing this? She wanted to try to manipulate me? What I wondered was whether she thought she could recruit me, or was this part of getting on Ryan's good side? Not that it would help. He was attracted to me, but that didn't mean he was interested. He could get any girl he wanted.

"There is nothing going on between us." At least not in the way Jackie meant. We were working together, but that wasn't what she was getting at. Not to mention we were working together against her.

"Come on, Nadia. We've known each other nearly our entire lives. You can't lie to me." What a hypocrite. I could barely take it.

"I'm not lying. There is nothing going on between us."

"Really?" There was an edge to her voice now. "So it's Dameon, then?"

"No!" I yelled louder than I meant. This probably wasn't playing it cool the way Dameon wanted us too. But then again, it was my normal reaction.

Jackie laughed. "Okay. Okay. I was just asking."

"Well, stop. This is ridiculous. I'm not here to have boyfriends." I would have been annoyed about that assumption even if I hadn't seen her in the woods. Seeing her only made things worse.

"I never said anything about boyfriends." She raised an eyebrow. "There is something called sex."

"Ugh. Stop it. You know I don't do casual sex." Not that I did any sex. I was a virgin and totally okay with that. There were way more important things in life that had nothing to do with sex.

"No. You don't," she mumbled. She knew the truth herself.

"What does my sex life have to do with anything?" I pulled the blanket up higher. Suddenly, my tank and shorts pajamas seemed revealing. I'd known Jackie forever, but was this really the same girl? I found it hard to believe.

"You need a sex life. That's the problem. Think of how much more productive you'd be if you had one."

"Because sex would help me with Meditation & Spiritual Release?" I threw out the name of the class I should have been studying for. With everything else going on, my schoolwork was being pushed to the back burner.

"Well, it will help you with a different kind of release." She raised an eyebrow. "And you know it will help with strength training. I mean it's quite a workout."

"Oh, because you're an expert on sex now?" I decided it was time to move the questioning on to her.

"Not an expert."

"Who are you, uh, learning with?" I wanted to sound natural, but it was hard. This was a conversation that should have been exciting. Instead, I felt like I was preparing for war.

"No one you know."

"Yet you say I'm the one with the exciting life?"

She smiled. "Okay. I may have met someone."

My stomach churned. I really hoped this wasn't when she told me she was sleeping with that disgusting leader. "What's his name?"

"Let's keep his name out of this." She ran her hand over the blanket. "It's not important."

"Wait. What?" I propped myself up more. "Why can't you tell me his name?"

"You don't know him, so why would his name matter?" She tried to sound nonchalant, but she failed.

"Because then I know who to pester you about."

She laughed. "Oh, in that case, call him Mr. Sexy."

"Yeah. No." Normally, I'd have laughed at Jackie for saying stuff like this, but not this time.

"Fine. I'll tell you his name, if you tell me which of your two potential partners you want more."

"Um, neither." I looked away.

"That's a lie and you know it." She laughed. "Come on now."

"Fine. Sure. It's a deal." I'd play along if it got me the information I needed.

"So who is it?" She leaned in close.

I tried not to recoil even though she disgusted me now. "Name first."

She sighed. "Fine. His name is Edmund."

"Edmund, huh?" I searched my mind for any Edmunds I'd met or heard about. I came up empty outside of characters in books.

"Yes. Like I said, you don't know him."

"Okay. I'll give you that." But I would figure out who he was. If the name was even real, or if a guy even existed. It may have all been a big lie to get me talking.

"Your turn. Which one is it?" She grinned.

Because I assumed she had lied, I lied too. "Dameon."

"Wait. What?" Her eyes widened. "You can't be serious."

"Why not? He's hot. He's got a great accent."

"Yeah, but he's not Ryan Grayson."

"Obviously... but when have I ever showed interest in Grayson?" There was only one answer. Never. I'd been very careful to keep my thoughts about him very private.

"Grayson? You always call him Ryan."

"So? What's the problem if I'm using his last name now?" I'd slipped up, and it was a mistake.

Jackie made a clicking sound with her tongue. "Come on. You know I've read your diary."

"What?" I pushed the blankets away and sat up straight. "You did what?"

"You know I'm a curious person."

"You read my diary?" Maybe in the big scheme of things it wasn't a big deal, but it still made me seriously mad.

"You can't be surprised." She pulled a stray string from the blanket.

"I am." I have so many personal things in there.

"Fine. Be surprised. But I read it. If you didn't want me to, you should have made yours digital like everyone else does. You want Ryan."

Digital diaries were even more ripe for invasion. And by more people. They were also easy to share and had the potential to go viral with an accidental click. I took my chances with the old-fashioned paper route.

"Well, that was before I met Dameon." I didn't enjoy lying, same as I didn't like pretending to have a crush on Dameon, but I had to throw her off my trail.

"Really? I'm sorry, but I'm struggling with accepting this. Ryan finally shows interest in you, and you don't want him?"

"I was never that into Ryan." I really hoped she dropped it, but I knew I wouldn't get that lucky. Not with Jackie.

"You called him akin to a god." She smiled, quoting me.

I felt the blood rush to my face—half out of embarrassment and half out of anger. "That was just flowery speech."

"Oh? What about him being so much more than he pretended to be? How he's so intellectual, but no one sees it?"

"Stop. Do you realize how wrong it is that you're giving me a hard time about stuff I wrote in my private journal?" Jackie had already proven herself to be a horrible person by killing someone, yet this was what pushed me over the edge? I needed to get myself together.

"What I don't get is why you never told me." She smoothed out her hair. "I'm your best friend. Yet you never told me you were into him. All you ever did was complain about him."

"I didn't complain."

"True." She tipped her head to the side. "But, you had no problem when I did."

"And you wonder why I didn't tell you anything?"

"No. I know why. You didn't tell me because you didn't trust me. I wish you trusted me more."

"You want me to trust you after admitting that you've read my diary without permission?"

"Is there another way to read a diary? I mean no one reads one with permission."

"Not true. Had you asked, maybe I would've let you read it."

She laughed. "Yeah right. Not a chance."

"So, tell me more about Edmund." I had to at least try to push things back on her.

"Not much to tell."

"Oh, come on. You lost your virginity, and it's not a big deal?"

"Who says I lost my virginity to him?" She pulled her leg up under her.

"Wait. There's someone else?" A lump formed in my throat. How much was she hiding from me? Compared to the whole murder thing, this shouldn't have been such a big deal, but we'd been best friends forever. Finding out she'd been hiding such important details of her life from me stung more than a little.

"Fine. I lost my virginity to him." She sighed.

"So tell me about it."

"The sex itself wasn't great." She pulled her other leg up, so she was sitting cross-legged. "The first time, I mean. But that was my fault. Not his."

"What makes you say that?" I tried to sound interested, because despite everything, I was. We'd talked about this. Sex. Virginity. We'd had these conversations so many times.

"Because he's way more experienced than I am."

"He's older, then?" I tried to imagine losing my virginity to an older guy. Experience could be good, but it would intimidate me.

"Yes."

"How much older?" I knew these sorts of details were private, but I needed to know.

"Does it matter?"

"Not really. Age is just a number. I'm just curious."

"He's a lot older. But I'm eighteen. It's okay."

"Age is just a number."

"Exactly." She nodded. "It doesn't matter."

"I meant being eighteen doesn't automatically change things."

"But, I mean I'm legal."

I really hoped he wasn't in his forties or older—not that any of it really mattered.

"Legal? How old is this guy?"

"Twenty-five."

"Okay... not awful old." A much smaller age differ-ence than I was expecting.

"But old." Old might have been stretching it, but twenty-five did sound way older than eighteen.

"He doesn't look old. He looks hot. And sexy." She smiled. For a brief moment, she reverted back to the Jackie I knew. Not the one who killed people.

"Will I meet him sometime?"

"Maybe." She shrugged.

"Only maybe?" That in itself was a warning sign. Even if I hadn't already known so much, she should have been excited at the thought of introducing him to me. It was how best friends worked.

"Eventually, I think you will. Okay, enough talk of Edmund... tell me more about why you want Dameon over Ryan. It makes no sense." Her eyes flashed with curiosity.

"Why do you care? You don't even like Ryan." I held her stare.

"I like him better than Dameon."

"What do you have against Dameon?"

"He's arrogant, for starters."

"Isn't that why you hate Ryan?" I couldn't let her get off that easy.

"I don't hate Ryan."

"Come on, Jackie. I thought we were being honest tonight." She'd complained about him constantly the past few years. It was part of why I never admitted my feelings for him. The other reason was I didn't want to admit them to myself. Putting those thoughts in a diary was one thing. Saying them out loud was something else altogether.

"He just annoys me. He's walked around like the king of the world since we were kids."

"You say that, but why? What did he ever do? I mean everyone fawned over him. Like Lauren and Aliana. But what did he do in particular?" Because I was realizing that I'd pegged Ryan wrong. Sure, I had always wondered if there was more below the surface, but that was more fantasy than anything. I had wanted to believe he was more than a pretty face.

My heart kicked up at the thought of him.

He was the perfect mix of rugged and classically handsome. His lips were kissable. I knew this without ever having had the opportunity to brush mine against his. He was one of those guys you could just tell. I knew he'd be a biter too.

I stopped my thought flow before I fell even deeper into that fantasy.

"Maybe I was totally wrong about him." Jackie sighed. "Maybe I was jealous because our families will never be like his. But you know..."

"What do I know?"

"He's into you. Really into you. If you two mated..."

"Okay you have to stop trailing off dramatically."

She laughed. "Sorry. I'm getting ahead of myself. If you mated with him, you'd be a Grayson. And then I'd be best friends with a Grayson."

"I'm not mating with him." Not to mention that, even if I did, it didn't mean I'd necessarily change my name. I was proud to be a Hazel, and I didn't think I'd ever want to give that up.

"No? Because you want to mate with Dameon?"

"I thought we were talking about sex? Where does mating come in?"

"You don't do casual sex. Remember?" She arched a brow.

"I might?" I didn't. Jackie was right about that, but that didn't mean I would let her off easily.

Jackie laughed. "Whatever. You don't do it, just like I don't."

"Wait a minute. You want to mate with Edmund?"

She leaned in further, pressing her forehead against mine the way she used to do when we were kids and her parents were packing up to leave again. It was also what she did when my father got sick, and afterward when he healed but was never the same. It was what she did when she wanted comfort, or when she wanted to give it. "Yes. And I will. He's already asked me."

"Wow. That's fast."

"What's wrong with fast if you know it's the right

person?" She pulled her head away. I'd touched a nerve. I could see it in her eyes.

"Nothing." Sometimes, two wolves felt the connection so strongly they had to jump right into it in order to survive. Other times, it was a slow build that took years. The two had to be in the right place at the right time. No matter how it started, when it took over, there was no turning back. Once you mated, you mated for life. "There's absolutely nothing wrong with it as long as you're careful."

"I'm never careful." She scoffed.

I laughed because she was right. As quickly as the laugh came though, it died. My insides pinched tight as I realized I'd almost forgotten what I'd overheard her say.

She'd killed someone.

"I'll make sure I get through this in one piece, though." She flashed me a sad smile that had concern rushing through my veins.

A horrible thought occurred to me—was Jackie being controlled? By Edmund?

"Are you okay?" I asked.

She nodded. "I'm more than okay. You, on the other hand—"

"No. No turning this back on me. We need to finish with you first."

"There's not much else to tell." She stretched out next to me.

"So the first time wasn't amazing. What about after that?" I needed to keep her talking.

"It got better and better." She grinned. "It's amazing, Nadia. Amazing."

"And it's more than sex?"

"So much more." She sighed. "I'm in love." She pulled open the blanket to slip in next to me in my twin bed. "He's wonderful. So wonderful. You can't imagine."

"Why? What makes him so wonderful?" It should have worried me to have her lying next to me that way, considering what I'd heard her admit to. But it didn't. She wouldn't hurt me, and I knew it.

"He's strong. Assertive."

"So, you're into alphas. Interesting. I thought you were more of a beta girl."

"Maybe that's the problem. I thought I was too, but I was wrong." She curled up on her side facing me. "We grow up believing one thing about ourselves just to discover we were wrong and are totally into something else entirely."

"So he's an alpha in bed or in real life?"

"He's an alpha everywhere."

"He doesn't hurt you, does he?" I had to ask. No matter what bad things she'd done, she was still Jackie. She was still my best friend. Ugh. How was I unable to accept that she wasn't the same person anymore? Maybe it was because deep down, I wanted to believe there had to be more to the story.

"Not unless I want him to." Her smile grew.

"Jackie!"

"What? Don't act like it's so crazy. Plenty of wolves like the pleasure and pain mix. Plenty of humans do too."

"So you're talking sex? Because that's different. I don't think I could ever mix the two, but in theory, I get it." Life was full of enough pain as it is. Who wanted to add to it?

"He doesn't hurt me. He pushes me though. He pushes me to rethink my beliefs and desires."

"But you aren't losing sight of yourself, right?" Of course I knew she was. "I mean it's great that he challenges you, but not all of your beliefs and desires are bad."

"I'm not losing sight of myself, but I am becoming a better version of myself."

"I thought you were a pretty great version before." There was a reason we were best friends.

She snuggled closer. "You were about the only one who did. Even my parents didn't like me."

"That's not true. They love you." It hurt to hear her say that, even though I'd heard her utter those same words many times over the years.

"Then why haven't I seen them in a year?"

"Because they have important jobs." It was like being kids again. I was making the same excuses for people that really had no excuse for their actions.

"Their jobs are more important than me." She had used those same words many times over the years. By the age of seven, she'd been tired of being raised by nannies. She'd yearned for a normal family and practically lived at my house. Even though my parents weren't perfect by any stretch of the imagination, they were there. And to her that was perfect.

"It sucks how much they're away. They missed most of your childhood and that's their loss. Because you were such a crazy good kid. But don't let your anger at them shape your future. You've always been super independent. Are you sure you want to be with a guy who's trying to destroy that?"

"He's not destroying that." She moved away. "How can you say that when you haven't met him?"

Maybe because he'd brainwashed her into hating humans. But I couldn't say that. And technically, I didn't know that he did. Maybe he introduced her to really bad friends? Or made her study weird books? Or...okay. He'd brainwashed her. Because otherwise, Jackie would still be Jackie. I knew it in every grain of my being. And maybe it wasn't too late to stop things. Sure she'd committed murder, but she could argue she did it under duress. She could find a way to be a better wolf and make up for it. Not that it made up for the loss of life.

Nothing could make up for the loss of life.

"Okay. Tell me more about him." I'd follow Dameon's advice. I'd play along. Strangely, it was easier than I expected.

*N*adia's brain was so unbelievably sexy. The way she connected details and jumped from one thing to another. I couldn't get enough of watching her work. I kept thinking the novelty of spending time with her would wear off, but as the days became weeks, and then more than a month, I only wanted more of her in any way I could get. It would never be enough. She could get enough of my watching her though.

"Quit staring and help me," she snapped. It wasn't the first time she'd snapped at me for that reason. And for one reason or another, I found it rather amusing. She was cute when she got annoyed.

But that didn't mean I wanted her angry. "How can I help?"

"Make calls. Everyone knows and likes you."

"But I can't tell them why I'm asking the questions. And I'll just make everyone suspicious." My last name carried weight, but it also made people nervous. They'd assume I was asking for some official business and start making calls of their own. This would mean my parents would get involved, and then we'd really be in trouble.

"True." She sighed, and rubbed at her neck as though it hurt her. "I just can't seem to find much."

"Just like Dameon said." And I hated that the guy was right.

"Come here." I gestured for her to join me on her bed.

"Why?" Her voice dripped with suspicion.

"Just do it."

"Okay." She sat down beside me.

I put my hands on her shoulders and started to give her a back rub. She sighed and leaned into me. "You're too stressed."

"That feels so good." She closed her eyes. "Perfect."

There were so many other things I wanted to do to her that would make her feel even better. But for now, I'd settle for the back rub. Her tank top left her shoulders bare, and I savored the sensation of my hands against her incredibly soft skin. How was her skin even that soft? It seemed impossible.

"Ryan?" She spoke my name so quietly.

"Yeah?"

"Did you know I had a crush on you?"

"What?" I tried to keep my cool. I'd known she felt something for me, but hearing her say so made it more real. "When?"

"For a while before we came here."

"Before we came here?" I continued to rub her back,

hoping it meant she would continue opening up to me. "We've only been here a month now."

"Yeah. And it was more than a month." She moaned softly. The back rub was really working. "I don't know why I'm telling you this."

"Thanks for telling me." I'd been waiting for some sign that she wanted more than the strange friendship-partnership we had. Normally, I would have pressed for what I wanted without waiting for her to make the first move, but I couldn't risk screwing things up. Not this time. Not with Nadia.

"So you aren't going to tell me that you had a crush on me too?"

"No." I turned her so we were looking at each other. "This is when I say I have more than a crush on you now." I leaned in and kissed her. I intended to keep it light, but when she arched into me, I knew that was impossible. I bit down on her lip, and she gasped, encouraging me to deepen the kiss and move into her mouth. Her hands moved into my hair, and I wrapped mine around her neck.

And then her door opened.

Nadia pulled away from me right as Jackie walked in.

Jackie grinned. "Uh, hey, you two. Am I interrupting something?"

"No. Nothing at all." Nadia jumped off the bed and looked at her phone. "I have to take this call. Be back." She darted from the room and closed the door.

I wanted to follow her and make sure she was cool with what had happened, but I was still in a stunned silence. That kiss had been more than a little bit incredible. And who knew where it would have gone if Jackie hadn't picked that moment to return to her room.

"Uh. I know I interrupted something." Jackie laughed. "You finally made your move?"

"Yeah. I guess I did."

"You guess you did?" She took a seat on her desk chair. "Either you made your move, or Nadia is even weirder than normal."

"Nadia is not weird," I immediately defended her.

"You are so gone over her." Jackie pulled a pack of gum from her desk, pulled out a piece, and popped it in her mouth.

"No kidding." There were two great things about Dameon's plan. One was that I had a perfectly good excuse to hang out with Nadia. The other was that playing along with things meant I could be honest about how I felt. The first was the more exciting part, but the second made everything easier.

"But she's gone over you too..."

"She had a crush on me, you know?" I figured Jackie had to already know this. "Before we came here."

"Oh, I know." She leaned back in her chair.

"She told you?" I looked at the spot that Nadia had just vacated. Our first kiss had been on her bed. Hopefully she was happy about that as the first place. I'd make sure it wasn't the only one.

"Not exactly. But it was easy enough to figure out." She smiled.

I knew she was hiding something, but it didn't matter. "If you say so."

"She's had a crush on you for years. We're best friends. It's my job to know these things."

"And is it your job to tell me these things?" I was flattered and happy to know this info, but I also knew Nadia trusted Jackie. Or well, she used to.

"No. It's not. I suck as a friend right now. But I really want you guys to get together." She slouched down in her chair and stretched her legs out.

"Trust me, I want that to, but I should probably go." I stood up.

"Wait. Before you do, I need to talk to you."

"Yes?"

She looked down at the floor and then back up at me. "I have an opportunity you might be interested in."

"An opportunity?" This was it. She was going for it.

"Yes. A group. A chance to join an organization I think would be a perfect fit for you."

"What kind of group?" I needed to keep my cool. I'd been waiting for this invite to come. It was our best chance for finding out what was really going on.

"It's a group of talented wolves dedicated to working together to help our kind." She sounded like she was reading from some brochure.

"A group of talented wolves? Right."

"Yeah." She nodded. "I think you'd really like it."

"I'm not sure I have time for it." I rubbed the back of my neck. Nadia claimed I did it when I was thinking deeply. I figured it would help to show Jackie I was thinking about it.

"Ryan, really. It won't take up too much of your time."

"What about Nadia? Could she join too?"

"I know you like her, but sometimes couples need to do different things."

"Oh, yeah?" I started for the door. "What about you? Do you do different things from your boyfriend?"

"I don't have a boyfriend." She stood up.

I gave her a long look.

"She told you!" Jackie yelled.

"You never talked about Nadia to your boyfriend?"

"Last time I checked, Nadia wasn't your girlfriend."

"Not yet." I smiled. "But she will be. I will make sure of it."

"Wow. There's that confidence back. I guess that was some kiss. It was a kiss, right?"

"It was *the* kiss. Not just a kiss." I put my hand on the doorknob. "And if you'll excuse me, I need to catch up with her."

"Wait. First promise you'll come. To the meeting."

"When is it again?" I feigned forgetfulness even though I was aware of the details.

"Three weeks. Friday night. Meet me at the edge of the woods, and I'll get you the rest of the way."

"What about Nadia?" I pushed again.

"Come yourself the first time. After that, we can bring her if you think she'd be a good fit. You seem to know her better than I do."

"Not better. Just differently." It was better. Much better, but I'd keep that to myself. We'd been playing along with things for over a month now. No reason to change it now.

"So you'll be there?"

"Yeah. I'll be there." I opened the door. "But I need to go."

"Fine. Go. But don't stand me up."

"It's not a date. I can't stand you up." I hesitated in the doorway, even though the only thing I wanted to do was find Nadia.

"You can always stand people up whether it's a date or not."

"Whatever you say." I headed out of the room to search for Nadia.

I'd hoped it would be easy to find her, but she wasn't in the lounge. I was pretty sure I knew where she'd gone.

I found her sitting under a tree in the woods. "Hey."

"Hey." She raked her teeth over her bottom lip. "So that happened."

"It did happen. I'm glad it happened."

"With everything else going on, can we really afford a distraction? I don't know about you, but I'm drowning in work. I didn't come to Lunar Academy to fail out."

"Because you really think that distraction will be worse than the tension that has been simmering?"

"We were doing fine with all the tension."

"Oh, yeah? It wasn't distracting at all?" I wasn't letting her off the hook that easily.

"Well, this will be more distracting."

"Why? It will just mean it's easier to get our stress out." I took a seat next to her.

"Get our stress out? I never said I was having sex with you."

"Did I say you were?" Of course I was thinking about sex. I'd been thinking about having sex with Nadia since move-in day. But that didn't have to happen yet. Just eventually.

"No, but I assumed that's what that stress comment meant."

"You know what they say about assumptions."

"I do know, so you don't have to remind me." I scooted closer to her. "Nadia. I can't help the way I feel about you."

"And I can't help how I feel about you either." She touched her neck.

I took her hand in mine. "Then let's stop holding ourselves back. It's only going to hurt us."

She didn't pull her hand away. "It can't hurt us."

"Sure it can." I traced circles on the top of her hand. "This is hurting me now. I need you, Nadia."

"I thought you said it isn't about sex."

"It doesn't have to be." I'd take whatever I could get.

"Then what do you need?"

"This." I kissed her again. This time I didn't pretend to make it soft and light. My kiss was hard and unyielding. She bit down on my lip, and I about lost it.

I let her take control, and that meant I somehow ended up on my back in the dirt with her on top of me. I didn't mind. I didn't mind one bit.

Then she stopped and looked into my eyes. "This is insane. I am insane."

She started to move off me, but I stopped her, wrapping my arms around her. "You're not insane. This is not insane. This is normal. Completely normal."

"Normal? You call this normal? I am lying on top of you under a tree."

"And the problem with that is what exactly?"

"Ryan." She said my name with annoyance, but it still managed to sound sexy.

"Yes, Nadia?" I ran a hand up and down her back.

"I shouldn't be doing this."

"You mean we shouldn't be doing this? Because this is kind of a joint activity."

"But I'm the one on top of you."

"Is that the problem?" I rolled us over so I was on top of her, but I was careful not to put too much weight on her.

"That wasn't what I meant."

"You sure?" I teased. I really liked teasing her.

"Yes."

"What view do you like better? I can't decide."

She laughed. "Really, Ryan? That's what you are going with?"

"What? I'm just wondering what your take is on positions."

"You don't need my take on positions."

"Why not? I care about your opinion." I brushed some hair away from her face. She was so beautiful—so fuckin' beautiful.

"This isn't happening again."

"Why not?" I was only half-heartedly asking, as I knew it would happen again. We had the kind of chemistry that couldn't be ignored.

"Because it shouldn't."

"Why not? Why in the world shouldn't it happen? And please don't say distractions because I've already dealt with that excuse."

"We shouldn't be together. That's why."

"Why shouldn't we be together?" Was she really going through the litany of excuses trying to find one that stuck?

"Because we shouldn't."

"Come on, Ms. Research. You know you need some supporting details to back you up."

"Because I'm scared," she whispered. "I'm completely and utterly terrified of what's going to happen."

"Well, that's a weak excuse if there ever was one."

"How is being afraid a weak excuse?"

"Because if we let fear guide us, we'd amount to nothing in life." It sounded like bullshit, and it probably was bullshit, but then again, it was also bullshit to call off something awesome because you were afraid. Fear wouldn't get either of us anywhere.

"That's ridiculous."

"Is it?"

"I can't do this. There is too much going on." She pressed her hands into the ground.

I released my hold on her but she didn't move.

"I never knew you were one for excuses."

"I'm not one for excuses. I'm one for reality."

"Then why don't we make the reality we want?" I was all for that.

"And what reality is that?" She moistened her lips.

"Any reality you want."

"I want to kiss you again." She stared at my lips.

"Then kiss me." I really hoped she listened. I didn't want to push her, but damn, I wanted her lips on mine again.

"Fine, but not because you told me to."

"Of course not." I smiled. She kissed that smile right off me.

*P*atience wasn't my virtue. Ryan had only left for the meeting thirty minutes earlier, and I was already losing it. I understood that sometimes you had to sit back and wait. It was required more often than not, but I hated it. I paced the edge of the woods like it was my job, following the same line again and again. It was times like this that my wolf instinct took over. She was begging to be set free, but I'd broken the no-shifting rule enough already this semester. I'd be good and follow the rules. It didn't mean I wasn't frustrated with having to stay back and wait. In theory, I understood why Ryan had to go first, but that didn't mean I liked it. Not one bit.

I'd grown more protective of him as time wore on. We'd been at school a couple of months now, and we were only getting closer.

I went into a lunge, stretching my tired body out. The October night was cool, but not cold. At least I wasn't sweating. Maybe I should go for a run in my human form. That would help me burn off my nervous energy at least.

"Hey, what are you doing out here?"

I straightened and saw Finn walking over. He wore jeans and a white t-shirt. Like me, he wasn't a huge fan of staying in his uniform more than he had to. "Lose a contact or something?"

"A contact?" I stopped short. "I don't wear contacts." I had perfect vision, like most wolves.

He laughed. "I know that. It was a joke. Usually you can take jokes." He'd been teasing me all semester, and generally it didn't bother me.

"Sorry. I'm tense." That was an understatement. I was ready to bite anyone who messed with me.

"Because of Ryan." Finn picked up a rock and tossed it into the woods.

"Possibly." I tried to pull myself together. I would give everything away if I wasn't careful. I looked up at the dark sky. The stars were dazzling as the moon was nearly nonexistent. Sometimes, I fantasized about what it would be like to get up in the stars, but astronaut training wasn't in the cards for me. There were far too many things I needed to do down on earth.

Finn laughed. "Possibly? Right. Because you aren't thinking about Ryan right now."

"Did he tell you where he was going?" I wasn't sure what excuse Ryan had used with Finn.

"Just some secret organization thing. Great that he invited me to go along." Finn laughed but it sounded forced. Understandably, Finn was hurt. It was strange seeing him hurt. He normally laughed everything off.

"He didn't take me either." I tried to make it sound like I was offended. I knew Ryan hated keeping Finn out of things, but there were too many people involved already. However, we all knew we'd have to bring him into the fold eventually.

"So, he ditched his best friend and girl for it. It must be good."

"His girl?" I really liked the sound of that. And well, it was true. Kind of. We'd kissed more than a few times since the woods, and I knew if I wasn't careful, it would go way beyond kissing. Did that make him my boyfriend? Was it okay to start using that label without talking about it first? Relationships were so complicated. Life was so complicated.

"Yeah, his girl. The guy is hopeless. You know that?" Finn craned his neck and looked up at the sky the way I'd been doing a few minutes earlier. "Putty in your hands. You better use that power wisely."

"Power? You notice I'm out here with you too." I leaned back against a tree. If someone looked out the Wolf Born dorm windows, they'd think we were having some clandestine meeting, but I didn't care. I was so over caring what anyone thought of me anymore.

"True... but if you'd really asked to go, he would have taken you. Unlike me." Finn didn't even try to laugh it off this time.

"Well, at least we are out here together." I felt for Finn. He'd always done everything with Ryan, and now he felt like he was being pushed aside. That couldn't be a good feeling.

"True. Very true." He came to stand closer to me. "The company helps."

"So did you finish your paper for Moon Phases?" I tried to make conversation that had nothing to do with Ryan.

"It's not due until Wednesday."

"Yeah. It's Friday." I pointed out the obvious. It was Friday, the beginning of the weekend. It should have been a fun night. Instead, I was stressed to the gills.

"I'll do it on Tuesday." He grinned.

I laughed. "Okay."

"Yours is done already, isn't it?" He ran his hand over the rough bark of the tree I leaned against.

"Not fully." My answer was truthful. There were still a couple of paragraphs that needed revising.

He gasped. "What? Is that possible?"

I smiled. I knew my reputation, and I didn't mind it. Most of me wished I could continue to live up to it, but there was so much going on. "I know. I've been busy."

"Busy with Ryan?" He wiggled his eyebrows.

I laughed. "That's part of it."

"Only part?"

"You know. College. It's busy."

"Things seem more normal with Jackie." He straightened and looked at me. "That's good, right?"

Normal probably wasn't the word I'd use. But it was a word. "Yeah. She was kind of crazy after the summer."

"Well, glad you guys are okay. There's no reason for

everything to change just because we're in college now." I knew he was really thinking of him and Ryan. "So, how late do you think this will go?"

"I don't know." I didn't, but I hoped it didn't go on too long.

"Then why are we waiting here?" Another smile spread across his face. This one was even bigger and toothier. It was trademark Finn really. He was a good-looking guy, but he also had this goofiness to him.

"I guess for no reason." Because I was obsessive and couldn't handle waiting inside.

"Want to go get a drink?"

"At Last Call?" I assumed he meant the local bar. There was nowhere to get alcohol on campus.

"Yeah. We'll be back in a bit, so you can resume your pacing."

I laughed. "Okay. That sounds good." I wanted to be around for Ryan, but I thought I might lose it if I stood there much longer. Not to mention we would eventually attract attention.

BEING A WOLF HAD ITS ADVANTAGES. One of them was you could drink at eighteen. The whole town was in on the secret of Lunar Academy and understood that the human laws didn't exactly fit for us.

We walked into the crowded bar. Thankfully, a smoking ban had come into place, so I wouldn't have to worry about leaving smelling like an ashtray.

The noise was overwhelming, but that made sense given the large crowd. My hope that I wouldn't run into anyone I knew was short-lived.

"Hey, guys!" Justine ran over to us. She was holding a glass that was mostly empty. "Finally, some more Wolf Borns are here."

"We aim to please." Finn grinned. "And I had to get Nadia off campus for a change."

"It's great to see you out." Justine linked her arm with mine. "Want me to introduce you to some people? There's some townies here in addition to students."

"First, she needs a drink." Finn linked his arm with my free one. "But we're not going anywhere."

"Suit yourself." Justine pulled her arm out from mine and skipped off.

"She's a funny girl." Finn watched her disappear into the crowd.

I shrugged. "We're all funny when you think about it."

"True enough." Finn walked over to the bar, and I followed. He turned to me. "What would you like?"

"Malibu and pineapple." If I was drinking, I might as well have what I wanted.

"You are such a girl." His nose wrinkled in disgust.

"Yes, I am a girl. Last time I checked." I hated when guys said things like that. I was proud to be a woman.

The bartender walked over. His brown hair was long, and a few pieces of it fell into his eyes. "What can I get you guys?"

Finn replied immediately, "I'll take my usual. She wants a Malibu and pineapple."

"It hurt you to say that, didn't it?" The bartender laughed.

"Kind of." Finn took a seat on a stool. "No offense, Nadia."

"Have you ever had a girlfriend?" I realized I'd never seen him with anyone before, and his reaction to my drink of choice seemed a bit overdramatic.

"Yes." He took his glass of whiskey from the bartender.

"Who?" I took my overly sweet drink. "Tell me."

"I'm not telling you anything." He took a long sip of his drink.

"Now you have to tell me. You can't pull that."

"Pull what?"

"Swinging the proverbial carrot in front of my face and then pulling it away." I shook my glass to watch the ice spin.

"It's not that exciting."

"Oh. I'm sure it is." I sipped my drink. "I'm sure it's very exciting." I wasn't entirely sure why I was pushing him, but I was. Somehow I needed to know.

Out of the corner of my eye I noticed a girl with dark hair and bright red lipstick slip behind the bar. She looked kind of familiar, and I thought she was another first year. I wondered how she'd managed to land a job at Last Call.

"If I tell you, you have to tell me something."

"What do you want to know?" Hopefully, it would be something stupid.

"I'll tell you that after I answer your question."

"Nuh uh. I'm not agreeing to answer you unless I know what it is." I wasn't that dumb.

"Live dangerously." He leaned closer to me. "It's fun. I promise."

"I prefer the safer route." I sat on the edge of my stool and watched. Justine was dancing with a girl I thought was Wolf Bitten. They were dancing close, and Justine was grinning. I wondered if they were more than friends, but now wasn't the time to ask.

"Boring." Finn downed his drink and placed it on the bar. The bartender seemed ready for it as he placed another one down immediately.

"Okay. Fine. Tell me. Who was it?"

"Donna Carrol."

"What?" I nearly spit out my drink. "You dated Donna Carrol?"

"Shh!" He scowled. "Keep it down. Don't completely ruin my reputation."

"Ruin your reputation? She's like a sex goddess. I heard she can do things that no one else can. And she's so much older. Isn't she like twenty-four? How would that hurt your reputation?"

"Because I like to seem somewhat respectable."

"You? Respectable?" I finished off my drink and set it on the bar behind me. "Oh, yeah."

"I'm respectable. I have to be."

"For Ryan?" Normally, I wouldn't have blurted it out like that.

"Yeah."

"Why?" I picked up the fresh glass that was already waiting for me. I probably should have stopped at one drink, but the first was so good. "I mean, I know he's your best friend, but why are you so worried about what he thinks and about your reputation?"

"I don't think you'd understand." He looked at the brown liquid in his glass before taking another swig.

"I could try." I took another sip of my drink. I was worried about Ryan. He hadn't called, which meant he was still at the meeting.

"Have another drink first." Finn gestured to my glass. I'd barely touched it. "Then I'll explain."

I took a few big sips. "Okay. I'm ready."

"So you know how important Ryan's family is." It wasn't a question. Everyone knew how important the Graysons were to the wolf shifter community.

"Of course." I picked up the pineapple garnish from my drink and took a bite.

"Well, my family has always been one step behind, you know?" He swirled the ice in his glass.

"Yes, I know." The one step behind description was pretty darn accurate.

"Well, being Ryan's best friend gives me a chance to change that." He downed the rest of his drink.

"Wait." I took another long sip. "You're friends with him to help your family?"

"Of course not." He slammed his empty glass down

on the bar. "But being helpful to him makes a difference for me."

"Got it. And that's why you care about your reputation. So let me guess, you aren't as dumb as you pretend to be?" Was the goofiness just a cover?

He shrugged. "You can decide that for yourself."

That was what I hated the most about the world I lived in. Everything was for show. A carefully designed veneer that often had no substance. It was all about power and money and pretenses.

I downed the rest of my drink and set it down. I was tipsy now. I'd skipped dinner, and two drinks on an empty stomach was a big mistake.

"Ready for your question?" He leaned back on his elbows.

"Sure." I wasn't ready, but there was no reason to put it off.

"Do you see yourself mating with Ryan?"

"Uh, yeah. Not going there." I took a few more sips of my drink.

"Why not?"

"Because that's super personal." I took another few sips, and before long, the glass was empty.

"Doesn't have to be."

"Mating is always personal. Super personal."

He nodded. "Want to do karaoke?"

"Karaoke?" That was an abrupt conversation change. "Are you crazy?"

"Why would that be crazy?" He tapped the bar, and the bartender brought fresh drinks for both of us. I hadn't asked, but I assumed Finn would pick up our tab. I was pretty short on spending money compared to most of my peers.

"Because I don't do those things." Just like I didn't get drunk on a Friday night with my maybe boyfriend's roommate. But here I was doing just that.

"Okay. fine. Then answer my question. It's your choice. Mating or karaoke?"

I picked up drink number three. I was crazy and knew I'd regret both the drink and my answer, yet I found myself taking a sip and answering. "Karaoke it is."

"Great. But to be nice, I'll go first." He leaned over to the bartender then walked over to the makeshift stage.

I settled in to watch as Rod Stewart's *Do Ya Think I'm Sexy* piped out.

Finn started to belt it out, and I practically fell off my stool with laughter. A few seconds later, he ripped off his shirt. I clapped along with the rest of the bar. He was in far better shape than I realized. But then again, most wolves were. It didn't take trips to the gym to get muscle definition.

"You should probably get your boyfriend down from there." A girl with bright purple hair sat next to me. "He's about to get clawed by some of the women in here."

"He's not my boyfriend. He's actually my boyfriend's roommate." And there. I'd used the word boyfriend out loud. It felt surprisingly good and natural.

"Oh man, that's bad."

"What do you mean?"

"You're out getting drunk with his roommate?" She

started to braid her hair, and I noticed there was some bright red color in there too.

"He's busy at a meeting I couldn't attend." I was drunk. Completely and utterly drunk. Finn was still hamming it up on stage. He was so fearless. I wanted to be fearless like him.

"Did you ask to go with him?" She finished the braid and used a bright blue hair tie at the bottom.

"Not really." I couldn't exactly explain the situation to this random girl.

"Then whose fault is that?" She moved to the other side of her hair and once again started to braid.

"No one's. This is no one's fault. Well, maybe my roommate. She invited him." I looked down at my glass; it was almost empty. I held onto it. If I set it down, I'd probably get a refill.

"He's out with your roommate and you are out with his. Maybe you guys should look into swinging." She tied her other pigtail.

"No, I only want my boyfriend." Boyfriend. There I went again. I had to get used to using that word. At least I hoped I needed to get used to it.

"Well, he seems to want you." She pointed to Finn.

"Nah. He'd never hurt Ryan." He was only being friendly. I was sure of that.

"Ryan?" She did a double-take. "You don't mean Ryan Grayson, do you?"

"Never mind." Great. I had to go and open my big mouth. I decided to fill my mouth with the rest of the drink.

"No. Wait. You are Ryan Grayson's girlfriend?"

"Yes." The cat was out of the bag. And I figured he wouldn't really care about my using that word. And if he did? He could set the record straight himself.

"Your turn." Finn grabbed my hand and tugged me toward the stage. "I picked a great one for you."

"What is it?"

"Just wait and see."

When Kylie Minogue's *Can't get You Out of My Head* came on, I automatically started to sing.

Maybe karaoke wasn't so bad.

RYAN

This felt like the beginning of a movie. I was following a girl I definitely didn't trust deep into the woods. In theory, I knew what I was in for, but that was just a theory, not reality. My wolf went along with it because he was happy to be set free. The no shifting rules were stifling his style.

We ran deeper into the woods, and then just as Nadia had described, there was a thick haze that seemed to come out of nowhere. I could feel the magic as I ran through it neck and neck with Jackie. I could barely see a foot ahead of me as we ran through the mist. Then just as suddenly as we entered it, the mist lifted and we were in a deeper, denser section of forest.

Jackie didn't stop. She kept running until she reached a clearing. She immediately shifted into her human form and dressed. I followed suit, glad when she held out a pair of pants to me.

I was fine being naked, but not if everyone else was dressed.

"Everyone knows who you are and that you're coming. You don't have to be nervous." She adjusted her skirt, so the buttons were facing the front.

"I'm not nervous." I buttoned my jeans.

"You're acting nervous."

I hadn't bothered with a shirt, but I figured that wouldn't be a big deal. "I'm not."

"Okay, then."

"I wish you would have let me bring Nadia." No reason to beat around the bush.

"Can't stand to be apart from her for even a few minutes?" Jackie rolled her eyes. "I never thought you'd be that guy, Grayson."

"It's not that." But even if it was, who the hell cared? I could do whatever I wanted.

"Oh?"

"It's just that you're her best friend, so this feels weird." I was getting tired of having to lie. Hopefully, this would be the beginning of putting this whole thing behind us.

"She didn't seem too upset." Jackie pulled a hair tie off her wrist and pulled her hair back away from her face.

"I think she did a good job of hiding it."

"Nah. Nadia can't hide things."

I held back a laugh. She was doing a pretty great job keeping the truth from Jackie. "Whatever you say."

I sensed the other wolves before I saw them. They were all in human form, more or less dressed, although most of the men were shirtless. I wasn't the only one who decided to bring as little as possible.

A tall, slender man with a heavy beard walked over to me. "Mr. Grayson. Thank you for joining us."

"I don't really know what this is or why you want me, but Jackie seemed to think I needed to be here." I played as dumb as possible. I wouldn't show any cards unless I had to.

The man nodded. "We will be happy to answer any of your questions while you're here."

He wanted to play nice? I would too. "Okay. Let's start with who are you?"

"My name is Carver. I run the Elite presence at the Lunar Academy."

"So this isn't everyone?" I looked at the assembled group. There were about a dozen of them—mostly men and three or four women.

"Not at all. This is only one local group," Carver explained. "There are many more of us, I assure you."

"Got it. And what do you Elites do? Secret rituals? Sacrifices?"

"No." Carver laughed. "We're dedicated to ensuring the survival and success of the wolf-shifter population."

"And how do you do that? I mean, aren't all of us dedicated to that cause?"

"We believe the time has come to step out of the shadows. We've lived in fear of the humans for long enough."

"So what do you want to do, kill them?" I tried to make that loaded statement sound as casual as possible.

There was silence. Complete and utter silence.

Finally, Carver spoke. "Of course not."

So they were lying? Cool. Because that was helpful.

"What would give you that idea?" Jackie looked at me like I had two heads. Was she serious?

"I don't know. I just wasn't sure how you expected to deal with the humans if they weren't happy we were revealing ourselves." Maybe I'd gone into the whole killing thing too early. I'd wanted to try to fit in, but that had been a misfire.

"We plan to explain that going along with us is in their best interest."

"And why would it be in their best interest?" Because talking always got you exactly what you wanted. I searched the faces of the others to see what the joke was.

"Because it is."

"Tell me more about this little group." I needed to get rid of the awkwardness. I'd screwed up somehow. I couldn't go back to the others without fixing this.

"First of all, it isn't little."

"It isn't?"

"No. Not at all. We already told you that. Haven't you been paying attention?" a girl asked. She gave Jackie a look that said, who is this idiot?

"Okay. And how do you work with the larger organization?" I really needed to fix this. I wasn't exactly making a good impression.

"We have representatives all over." Carver spoke slowly like he was afraid I couldn't follow. "And we use the representatives to share information for recruitment and planning."

"And we try to make sure no wolves get in our way," the annoyed girl from earlier spoke. "Contrary to what you seem to believe, not everyone of our kind wants what's best for us."

"What wolf would be against our advancements?"

"There are always ones with strange agendas." Carver rubbed his hands.

"Oh." I tried to play it cool this time. "And are there any of these wolves here at the academy?"

"Yes." Jackie let her word hang.

Keep it cool. Keep it cool. I repeated the mantra in my head.

"You have some in your house," Carver added. "More than one."

"Really?" I kept my expression neutral.

"Yes."

"Who?"

"We can't tell you unless we know you can be trusted." Carver was speaking extra slowly again.

"I thought you wanted me here. You were the ones who invited me."

"We did invite you." Annoyed girl walked over to join Carver right in front of me. "We know you have a lot to offer." She didn't look like she necessarily believed that anymore.

"Then tell me." I was done being talked to like an idiot. I was a lot of things, but stupid wasn't one of them.

"One is Dameon." Jackie gave me a long, intense

stare. "Not that it should surprise you. It was odd he was here to begin with."

"Yes. That guy is odd." At least I could be honest about that. I'd grown to feel okay about him, but that didn't mean I didn't think he was weird.

"We have reason to believe he may be trying to recruit you as well."

"Recruit me?" I laughed. "No. Not exactly."

"Are you sure?" Jackie narrowed her eyes. "He hasn't talked to you about anything?"

"No." I shook my head. "I mean he annoys me. But nothing about stopping you." I was outright lying, but I had no choice.

"I think he's gone straight to Nadia." Jackie turned to Carver. "I think he has his claws in her."

What? Jackie was throwing Nadia under the bus already? "No. Absolutely not. If he was, I'd know. Nadia and I spend lots of time together."

"Are you in a relationship?" annoyed girl asked.

"Yes," I answered immediately. "So I would know."

"Something is going on there." Jackie pursed her lips.

"Is this why you didn't want to bring her?" If Jackie wanted to play things that way, I wouldn't just sit back.

"What do you mean, she didn't want to bring her?" Carver frowned.

"I wanted to bring Nadia, and Jackie didn't want me to." It was the truth. I'd asked to bring her multiple times.

"I said I thought he should come alone first. I had to use my discretion. Particularly because I believe she may be involved with Dameon's mission," Jackie spoke quickly, as if struggling to get her excuse out fast enough.

"She isn't." Maybe I was jumping too fast to defend Nadia, but I couldn't help it. It came naturally. "I can assure you she wants nothing to do with him."

"If you say so." Jackie rolled her eyes. She did that entirely too much.

"I know so."

"So what do you say?" Carver gave me a serious look.

"Say to what?" I'd missed something. That wouldn't help my case for arguing I was smarter than I was being given credit for.

"Will you join our cause?" the annoyed girl asked. "That is why we asked you here."

Maybe I should have asked for her name, but I figured it didn't really matter. "I need to know more about it still. In theory, I agree with what you say you support, but I'm not going to take your word for it."

"You need to be initiated before we tell you more. And that initiation needs to happen soon." Carver was talking normally to me again at least.

"Well, I'm not getting initiated into anything without more information." They were crazy if they thought I'd do that.

"Is he always this difficult?" Carver turned to Jackie.

"Yes." Jackie nodded. "But that's part of his desirability. Everyone knows he doesn't enter into things willy-nilly. That's why I wanted to get him here first. Before I brought in the twins. They will follow as long as he does it."

I imagined Nadia listening to this. She and North would follow because I did something? That was laughable. Very laughable. "I'm not so sure about that, but whatever you say."

"Time is of the essence here." A guy with jet-black hair and yellowish eyes walked over and put his arm around Jackie. "We can't waste it."

"So, this is the famous Edmund, then?" Jackie hadn't told me much about him, but I was well aware of his existence.

"Famous?" Edmund turned his head to look at Jackie. "You been talking about me, darling?"

"Nothing more than I should have been." Jackie laughed in a forced way.

He patted her shoulder. "You're not in trouble. I was just wondering how much he knew about me."

Not in trouble? What the hell was this? "I don't know much. I only know the two of you are together, and you're the one who introduced her to this illustrious organization."

"I like this kid." Edmund pointed at me.

"I'm not a kid."

"I'll call you a kid until you're initiated. How does that sound?" Edmund gave me a condescending smile.

"I'm not getting initiated without Nadia and North. How does that sound?" I didn't like anything about this situation. I wanted to regroup and try again.

"Ryan." Jackie slipped out from under Edmund's arm. "Can we have a word for a moment?"

"What?" I looked at my wrist even though I wasn't

wearing a watch. I couldn't wear one easily when I shifted to my wolf. "What do you want to have a word about?"

She walked off from the others, dragging my arm to get me to come with her. She stopped and hissed at me. "I thought you would give this a chance."

"I am. I showed up. However, I don't like the way you're dismissing Nadia. I'm not doing anything unless she's involved." I folded my arms over my chest. Maybe it seemed like a childish move, but I didn't give a shit. I meant what I'd said.

"You know you can still be together even if she doesn't join, right?" Jackie sighed. "Because if that's what this is about, you're being ridiculous."

"If you're correct and she's being recruited by a rival organization, it's okay?"

"I didn't say she was actually joining, just that she's being recruited. That's something altogether different."

"I already told you all I have to say." I stepped back from her.

"So that's it? You're leaving?"

"Yes. Is there a problem?" I'd already been there long enough. I had a feeling Nadia was getting worried.

"No." Carver walked over to join us. "You can leave. We will wait if we have to, but we would like your help with our cause."

"Good." I changed out of my pants and shifted back to my wolf, letting his strength surge through me, before running back toward campus. I changed, found the clothes I'd hidden, and immediately pulled out my phone to call Nadia. I was surprised she wasn't waiting for me outside. Maybe she wasn't as nervous about things as I'd thought.

"Hey!" Nadia picked up immediately. "Ryan! I miss you!"

"Hey... you sound drunk." I'd never heard or seen Nadia drunk. To say I was surprised was an understatement.

"I am drunk. I shouldn't have had so many drinks, but they were so good!"

"You got drunk tonight? While I was at that meeting?" This wasn't like Nadia at all. And who the hell was she getting drunk with? I felt my wolf growl. He didn't like this anymore than I did. Maybe we hadn't officially declared ourselves a couple, but I hoped she wasn't off with Dameon. The only other person she'd have normally gone out with was Jackie, and she'd been with me tonight.

"It's all Finn's fault."

"You are with Finn?" I felt better. I didn't necessarily like the jealousy that was surging through me but at least I felt better when I figured out who she was with.

"Yes! I did karaoke!"

"You did karaoke?" Was this the same Nadia?

"Yes!" Admittedly, she sounded ridiculously cute and excited, but that didn't make up for how worried I was.

I needed to see her. "I'm on my way."

"How did it go?" she asked.

"Uh, I'll tell you about it when I see you." I didn't even know where to begin.

I found the boots I'd stowed and headed down the road to the bar. It didn't take me long to find her dancing with a couple of girls I vaguely recognized.

I put my arms around her from behind. She spun around. "Ryan!" She wrapped her arms around my neck. "I am so happy to see you!"

"I'm happy to see you too, babe."

"Babe?" She put her hands on my shoulders. "You never call me babe."

"Do you mind if I call you that?"

"No." She shook her head. "Not at all."

"Hey, man." Finn walked over. "How'd the super special meeting go?"

"You got her drunk?" I tried to lower my voice so Nadia wouldn't hear. She seemed to be more interested in the music anyway.

"Not on purpose. But she was all upset that you went to that stupid meeting without her." He took a swig from his glass.

"It was her who was upset?" I knew he was pissed. He had every right to be.

"We both were." Finn shrugged. "And I've been looking out for her. Of course."

"I appreciate that." I did. I appreciated him more than he realized.

"Ryan." Nadia rested her head on my chest.

"I think I should get her home." I put my arm around her. "You staying out?"

"Yeah, I'll see you later." Finn gave a half wave before disappearing into the crowd.

Nadia could barely walk a straight line, so I gave her a piggyback ride to the Wolf Born dorms. She giggled the whole time.

"This is so much fun!" She talked louder than she needed to. It had me questioning if she'd ever been drunk before. I'd definitely never seen it.

I made it back to her room. She handed me her key. I unlocked the door and she stumbled in, tugging me over to her bed.

"Make love to me, Ryan. Now. Please." Her eyes were wide and bloodshot. A reminder of how much alcohol flowed through her veins.

"Sorry, babe. Not tonight." I tried to sound as nice as possible. Having sex with Nadia was high on my to-do list but not like this. She was trashed.

"You don't want me?" Her bottom lip quivered.

"Of course I want you." I pulled her into a hug. "Just not when you're drunk. I won't let our first time be this way. I can't." I listened to myself. Was this really me? Was I really turning down an opportunity to have Nadia?

"But I want you." She wrapped her arms around my neck.

"Oh, babe. I want you too. I want you more than you'll ever know, but not like this."

"You're no fun."

"Nope. I'm not. But I don't want you to ever have any regrets." I brushed her hair back from her face.

"I won't." She ran her lips down my neck.

I tried to pull back. "You might."

"Ryan?" She rested her head on my chest again.

"Yeah?"

"I love you. I mean, I am in love with you."

I felt something. A surge of something in my chest. "I love you too, Nadia." I kissed the top of her head and helped her into her bed. I pulled the blanket up on top of her. "You may not remember this in the morning, but I will."

I walked out of her room and closed the door. I'd either made the biggest mistake or the best decision of my life. I really hoped it was the latter.

"*W*hy are we here again?" Ryan whined while we waited in the main lounge of the Wolf Blood dorms. I knew he was complaining out of discomfort, and I couldn't blame him. I didn't love standing inside a dorm full of half-vampires either. Although knowing Ryan, he was more concerned about being in the dorm of another house rather than their abilities. He didn't think anyone was as strong as we were. And in brute strength that was true, but I wasn't about to screw with the Wolf Bloods either. After a few months at Lunar Academy, I'd learned to beware of all the houses for different reasons.

"Because we need help, and rumor has it this Lee guy is supposed to know something about the Elites." I whispered their name, not wanting anyone else to hear.

I'd already gone through my usual connections, both on campus and off, and as Dameon had predicted, I kept hitting dead ends. No one knew about the group.

At least, they weren't admitting to.

Since they were breathing down our throats about initiation, we didn't have any time to waste. I loved Ryan had put his foot down and asked North and me to be included, but we still needed more information on the Elites before any of us agreed to take part in what they were doing. I'd overheard Jackie mention Lee's name to Edmund in a couple of their phone conversations she thought I was asleep for recently, and figured he might be our shot at learning more.

"We don't need his help." Ryan kissed my forehead. "You're the best."

"You have to stop thinking that. I know I'm good at researching things, but I'm not the best." I had plenty of confidence, but I was also a realist who could admit when she needed to outsource some help.

"Is this about that A- you got on your paper?" He slung his arm over my shoulder. "Because an A- isn't all that bad."

"No, it's not about a grade. Don't be ridiculous." I looked at my watch. What was taking Lee so long? He was supposed to come get us. We'd agreed on three o'clock since he said his roommate wouldn't be in at that time. Apparently, he had a class on the other side of campus until four.

Two Wolf Bloods slipped through the dormitory doors. Their eyes skimmed us, but thankfully neither asked what we were doing here. I shivered once they started up the stairs. Ryan wasn't the only one who was uncomfortable.

"Don't be ridiculous? You cried," he said, pulling me back to our conversation. If the sight of those two had unsettled him any, he didn't let it show.

"I didn't cry." I looked at my watch again.

Where was this guy? I didn't want to stand here any longer than we had to.

"You cried. Don't lie." Ryan nuzzled my neck.

"No, I got teary because I was disappointed in myself." I never left things to the last minute, yet I had when it came to that paper. That seemed to be an all too frequent occurrence now. "There's a difference."

His head cocked to the side. "Is there? Enlighten me."

"Yes. The two are completely different. Crying implies lots of big tears spilling down your face, and you often lose your breath."

He pulled me into a hug, a lopsided grin on his face. "And that's what I love about you, babe."

"You know I shouldn't like you calling me babe." I smoothed my hand down his toned arm.

"Why is that?" His lips pressed against my neck.

I stiffened. Was he crazy? He was kissing my neck in the middle of the Wolf Blood lounge?

I laughed like the sensation tickled, and shifted away from him. Thankfully, he didn't seem offended. "Because, it's like you're calling me less or something."

That wasn't entirely true. I liked the endearment coming from Ryan. The problem was that I knew I shouldn't. I never would have tolerated it from anyone else.

"Where's that coming from?" He spun me so I was

looking at him, and put his hands on my hips. His brows pinched together as a serious expression took over his face. "I take it you don't remember what was said the night when you got drunk, then?"

I blinked. "Not really."

"You don't remember anything from that night?"

My cheeks heated. "Should I?"

Crap. Hopefully, I hadn't said or done anything stupid.

"Well, probably. But it's fine." He kissed my forehead. "Don't worry about it."

But I would worry about it. Had I been that drunk? Most definitely. I was still mad at myself for it too. Between that and my school studies, I was acting so far from my normal self that it was crazy. Then again, I was also doing whatever it took to figure out more about the Elites and what they were up to. Research. That was why I was here. I was researching more about them. So, maybe I hadn't lost myself completely.

Footsteps on the stairs caught my attention. I glanced that way, hoping it would be Lee.

I knew what he looked like, simply because I'd looked him up, and the two people coming down the stairs weren't him.

"What are you Wolf Borns doing here?" the guy snapped. His eyes were dark and menacing. The girl with him placed a hand on her hip and gave Ryan a once-over.

Ryan turned and positioned himself in front of me. It was a protective stance, but one I was okay with given the circumstances. "We're waiting for Lee."

"Lee?" The guy narrowed his eyes. "Lee who?"

"Twain," I said.

"Are you serious?" the girl asked with a chuckle. "Lee Twain has guests?"

"Yes." While I might not know the guy, I still didn't think he should be laughed at. "Is that a problem?"

"No, not at all." The girl's eyes slid over to Ryan. "It's just not every day Ryan Grayson walks into Wolf Blood. Especially not to see Lee Twain."

Of course her focus was Ryan. I wondered if I would ever get used to being an afterthought to other people when I was around him. It was something I'd have to accept if I wanted to be with him.

"He's on the fourth floor," the guy said, his upper lip curling.

The girl slapped him on the chest. "You can't just send them up."

"Why not?"

"Because this is our turf. No one wants a couple of Wolf Borns snooping around." Her eyes shifted between us, her dislike of the idea evident.

"Exactly. They'll be watched." The guy laughed before he grabbed her hand and pulled her with him to the exit.

I tried not to worry as we made our way up the stairs. No one would mess with us and risk expulsion. Right?

"How are we going to find his room?" I asked as we walked down the hall of the first-year Wolf Blood men's hall.

"We'll figure it out." He draped his arm over my

shoulder as we walked past a few guys dressed in athletic shorts giving us the eye. I recognized one of the three from my Meditation & Spiritual Release class.

He nodded, and I flashed him a small smile.

We continued down the hall. Most of the doors were closed. I had my doubts we'd find Lee's room, until I overheard a guy mention his name.

"I'm just gonna ask him for his Essential notes. Two seconds. That's all it's gonna take," the guy said.

The other guy huffed. "Dude, we have to go. I'm meeting Stella in the quad."

"Two seconds." The first guy continued down the hall, pausing in front of one of the doors. He lifted his hand to knock, but the other guy strutted away.

"I'm leaving your ass, then."

The one at the door tossed his hands up. "Two seconds. Give me two seconds. There's a paper due next week. I need the notes."

"Get them tomorrow," the other guy growled. "We gotta go. Besides, Lee's weird. You know it won't be two seconds. He'll talk your ear off about his stupid comic book obsession."

"Damn, you're right." The guy stepped away from the door, and jogged down the hall to meet his friend. Neither of them seemed to care we were there. I was glad.

"Guess we know where Lee's room is now," I said.

"Told you we'd figure it out." Ryan smiled, and I nudged his shoulder.

"That was pure luck, and not because of anything we did."

"Doesn't matter." He locked his fingers with mine and pulled me toward the door with him. He knocked.

"Yeah?" Lee called from inside.

"Uh, it's Nadia Hazel. We were supposed to meet today."

A shuffling of stuff came from inside and then footsteps. "Crap, is it three already?" he asked as he swung the door open.

"Yeah. A little after, actually." I softened my words with a smile. He looked rough. There were dark circles beneath his eyes and a slight amount of stubble across his jaw. Usually, he looked put together whenever I saw him in class.

"Sorry about that. I got sidetracked."

He motioned for us to step inside. When we did, I happened to notice the way he glanced around the hall before closing the door as though he was making sure no one saw us enter. A shiver slipped up my spine at the oddness of it.

"So, you think you know something about the Elites?" Ryan asked, getting straight to the point.

"Yes. Well, maybe." He ran a hand through his hair. It was then I noticed he wore a gray t-shirt with some cartoon-looking character printed on the front. He really did love comics. "They're a large group. One I'm beginning to think includes all houses. You obviously know something about them too, so I'm not crazy."

Something reflected in his eyes broke me. I hated he

thought he was crazy because of all this. "No. Not at all. Is there anything you can tell us about them that would indicate what their plans are?"

Lee thought for a moment. "Have you seen the tattoos? That's your first clue.""

"Tattoos?" Ryan released my hand to fold his arms over his chest. "What kind of tattoos?"

"Markings. I haven't figured out what they mean. Well, not exactly. They are a signifier that someone is part of the Elites though."

"Jackie did get a tattoo over the summer. It's on her shoulder."

"Shoulder?" Lee hurried to his desk. A folder sat open. Notes spilled out from it. "That's a new spot."

"Okay. So, tattoos. What else can you tell us?" There had to be something more. "Are they good? Evil?"

Lee glanced at me. His eyes darkened. "They're dangerous."

"We've gathered that much," Ryan said. I knew he was talking about Jackie having killed someone. "But we need more information than that."

"There isn't much more I can say right now." He glanced at his cell, clearly checking the time. "My roommate, Axel, will be here soon. He's not into this whole conspiracy, secret-group-hidden-among-us thing."

"Okay." Ryan dragged the word out.

"Can we set up another time? Like maybe later tonight?" If he knew something about their plans, he needed to tell us.

"Not tonight, no. I have, um, plans." He averted his

eyes from mine. Was he hiding something? "I'll have to touch base with you again some other time."

I sighed. "Okay. Thanks for your time." I took Ryan's hand and dragged him from the room. We walked back down the stairs and outside. I pulled in a deep breath to help calm my irritation. "He didn't seem to know much. That was a waste of time."

"No. We now know about the tattoos."

"What point did it prove?"

"That you are really good at what you do." He put his arm around me and pulled me into his side. "It's time for you to stop arguing with me about that."

"Are you ready to join the Elite?" Jackie tried on yet another dress. This was number five. She wasn't getting ready for anything Elite related. This evening was for an academy function: the winter party. I still couldn't believe the semester was over. The time had flown by in a way it never had in high school. Maybe it was true what they said about time moving faster the older you got. Or maybe it had seemed fast because life had been so busy and crazy.

"No." I ran through spell-check on a paper.

"Nadia."

"What?" I minimized the document on my computer. "You asked and I answered."

"Why not?" Jackie put a hand on her hip.

"Because, I still don't really get what it is I'm being initiated into."

"You like being a wolf?"

"Yes."

"You want wolves to continue doing well?"

"Obviously."

"Then you want to join. I promise." Jackie returned to the mirror and turned around, checking out her butt.

"You won't ask me to do things I don't want to do, are you?" I wasn't ready to drop the conversation yet.

"Why would you even ask that? I mean it's me we're talking about."

"And you've been super mysterious and strange since August. I mean I still haven't met your boyfriend."

"Well, you will if you join." She looked in the mirror and made a face.

"You look beautiful." I wasn't just saying that. She did. Although, it had nothing to do with the dress. She was glowing. I didn't like the idea of Edmund, but evidently, he was doing something positive for her.

"You said that about the last four dresses."

"Because they all looked beautiful."

"You just want me out of here so you can work."

"Maybe." I smiled. Despite everything, Jackie knew me.

"You have to go tonight."

"It's just a party. I don't have to go to a party." What I needed to do was finish this paper, so I could save my grade. No, an A- wasn't the end of the world, but I was a good student. I refused to ruin my GPA if I could avoid it.

"Ryan wants you to go."

"And that changes what exactly? He can go without me." Of course I didn't want him to. The thought of him dancing with anyone else upset me, but he had the right to. I didn't own him.

Jackie narrowed her eyes. "He's your boyfriend."

"So?"

"So. That means he won't go without you."

"Jackie, can I ask you something?"

"Sure." She spun in front of the mirror again. "But first, tell me, this dress or the one before it?"

"This one. The purple works for you." And I wasn't just saying that.

"Thanks. Okay. Ask away."

"Would you ever hurt someone?" I knew this was dangerous territory, but I had to ask.

"Hurt someone?" She blanched. "What kind of question is that?"

"I just." This was when I wished I could get this out. "I was wondering if you'd ever hurt someone."

Jackie knelt down in front of me. "What aren't you saying?"

"Nothing. Just forget I said anything."

"No." She put her hands on my knees. "I won't forget you said something. That's a really weird and pointed question to ask me. I don't believe it's random. It came from somewhere."

"No. It's random."

"Wait." Understanding crossed her face. "You... Oh

my gosh." She stood up. "Oh my God. You... You followed me that night, didn't you?"

"What? No." I shook my head. I hated lying. It was one thing to pretend but outright lying was almost impossible for me.

"You did... I knew something was off with you the past few weeks."

"I don't know what you are talking about." I looked down at the floor.

"Stop lying, Nadia." Jackie was pleading with me. "Please listen to me."

"I'm listening."

"What you heard..." She looked away. "I only did it because I had to."

"What?"

"Don't play stupid. That guy. The one I..." A single tear streamed down her face.

"Terminated." Jackie knew. She was right. There was no reason to pretend anymore.

"Yes. He killed a pup... I think Dameon is involved, which is why we need your help."

"There is no way Dameon killed a pup." So much about Dameon was still a mystery to me, but I knew enough about his character to believe that.

"Not him, but people he works with. You have to trust me."

"I don't know who to trust anymore." And I may have just blown everything. After months of keeping my mouth shut, I'd just completely shown my cards.

"It keeps me up every night." Jackie wrapped her arms over her chest.

"What does?"

"What I had to do."

"Why did you have to do it? Why not get the authorities involved?"

"He would have killed another pup. And he would have killed me."

"I don't know what I would have done in your situation. It must have been awful."

"You'd have done the same thing." Jackie pointed at me. "You wouldn't have allowed a child to get hurt."

"It's impossible to know what I would have done, but I would have tried to help a child. Yes." I knew that much, but could I have killed someone? I wasn't sure I had it in me.

I was confused. Overwhelmed really. And there was only one person who could help. But I refused to rely on him. I wouldn't be that girl who needed a guy. Especially not Ryan Grayson.

"It's going to be okay, Nadia. We will be part of something big."

"It's not supposed to be like this. It's supposed to be college. Fun times. Maybe some all-nighters studying. Not worrying about the fate of our kind and what side to be on." I closed my eyes, willing the craziness away.

"You really should come tonight. It's to celebrate the end of the semester."

"I'm staying in to work." For more reasons than not.

"Fine. But if I see Ryan, I'm sending him up. You

look really freaked out, and I don't think you should be alone."

"You don't need to worry about me. I should be more worried about you."

"And have you been? Or have you been afraid of me?"

"Maybe a little bit of both."

"I can't believe you've been afraid of me." There was real and true hurt on Jackie's face. "I can't believe you thought I was capable of killing in cold blood."

She started to laugh. Like really laugh. Almost fell over laughing. "What? Did you think I was running around hacking people up?"

"I don't know." I purposely avoided thinking about any of the details. I knew it wouldn't help.

"Were you afraid I would kill you?"

"No," I answered immediately. "I wasn't."

"Good." She picked herself up off the floor. "I'd never hurt you."

"I know." And not just because she thought I was useful to the Elites. Our friendship was more akin to family than friends. "I don't know how I know, but I do."

"Finish your work, then head out to the party. You have to live a little, you know? We're only young once." She slipped on a pair of silver stilettos and grabbed a purse before heading out of the room, shutting the door behind her.

I closed my document and picked up my phone. I texted Ryan immediately.

Please come here.

His response was immediate. **On my way.**

He must have really been on his way, because my door opened about a minute later. "Hey."

Relief flooded me. "Hey."

"You okay?" He leaned on the edge of my desk. "You look kind of pale."

"I'm fine. I think. But I kind of screwed up."

"I doubt it." He pressed his palms into the desk on either side of him. "But what makes you say that?"

"I asked Jackie about the termination."

He appeared to mull over what I said. "Wow."

"Yeah. She says the guy killed a pup and was going to kill another."

"Well, that makes more sense. It fits her and how that group has been acting." He rubbed the back of his neck. "This stuff all gets more convoluted by the second."

"She also said Dameon may be involved with them."

"I don't know what to believe anymore."

"Me either."

He took a seat on my bed. "Ever wish we could just forget this stuff? Even if for one night."

"Often." I walked over and sat next to him. Sometimes, I needed us to be close.

"But we can't."

"Not yet." I leaned back on my elbows and looked up at the ceiling. "Definitely not yet."

"You already have a plan brewing in that beautiful, sexy head of yours, don't you?" He leaned back next to me.

"Of course."

"Where are we going?"

"Dameon's room." I spit it out.

"Oh, I was hoping you weren't about to say that."

"Yeah, me too. But we need to find out more about him." We'd blindly followed him and his plan. It may not have been a huge mistake, but it was at least a small one. But we'd had no way to find out information. Everywhere we looked, we'd hit dead ends.

Ryan sat up. "I saw him on my way over here. So I know he's out of his room."

"Good." At least we wouldn't have to come up with a diversion to get him moving.

"You sure about this?" Ryan took my hand in his.

"No. But when has that ever changed anything?"

*D*ameon's door was locked. Not that I was remotely surprised. He was hiding things, and we needed to get to the bottom of it.

"How are we getting in?" Nadia let go of the doorknob after she established for herself that the knob was not turning.

"This way." I made quick work of the lock and pushed the door open.

"How did you know how to do that?" There was something akin to awe on her face.

"Eh, just something I know how to do." I shrugged it off. No need to go into some of the adventures Finn and I had had.

"That isn't an answer."

"No, it's not. But that's okay."

I walked in first, and Nadia stayed close by my side. The window by his bed was open, letting in a cold breeze.

"So what are we looking for exactly?" I flipped on the light switch. His room looked pretty normal. It was large, but no larger than my room. The only difference was he didn't have a roommate.

"I don't know." Nadia rested her chin in her hand. "We're looking for something. Anything."

"That's real specific."

She shrugged. "I'd be specific if I could."

We were careful. Very careful. If we did find what we needed, there was no reason to alert Dameon to it.

"Oh my God." Nadia held up a small object. She turned it around, and I saw it was an ID.

"That's Dameon." I took the small card from her. "But that's not his name."

"You think?" Nadia took the ID back. "Marshall Martin? And it's an Arkansas driver's license. Isn't he supposed to be from London or something?"

"It's got to be fake."

"Unless his whole Dameon story is." Nadia sat down on the edge of his bed. She picked up a book. It was super old and the cover was half off.

"Isn't that one of the books from the soundproof room?"

"Maybe." She handed it to me. It was open to a page. There was a list of names with red lines through them written on a piece of paper. "Do you think that's a kill list?"

"I'd say yes, but we fell for that kind of thing before. No more jumping to conclusions."

"But did you see the title of this book?" She closed it to reveal the cover.

"Warfare." I read the script font. "Okay. So something that Jackie said rings true. Dameon isn't as innocent as he wants us to believe."

"I don't even know what to do." She pulled the book close to her chest.

"Maybe we should stop." I didn't want to be the one giving up, but I also didn't want to be the one encouraging us to keep pushing ourselves deeper into a mess. "At least temporarily."

If it were just me I wouldn't have cared, but this wasn't just me. It was Nadia. And I knew I couldn't live with myself if anything happened to her.

"We can't let this go." She held out the book. "Or that." She pointed to the door, and I assumed she meant Jackie and the Elites. "Or this!" She held up the ID.

"This is too big." It seemed too big for everyone.

"Which is precisely why we can't let it go."

"You won't drop this no matter what I say, will you?"

"No. But you can. I'll be fine." She flicked the piece of paper with the red lines again.

"Are you kidding?"

"I'm fully capable." She put a hand on her hip.

"I know you're capable. Hell, you're more capable than I am. That doesn't mean I'm leaving you to handle this alone." I wasn't ditching her. No question about that.

"We have to do this, Ryan." Her brown eyes were so wide. "You and I both know that."

"But not alone. We are in over our head. We have to get help."

She nodded. "I know. We've done what we could do."

The door swung open, and Dameon walked in. "Well, hello there. I wasn't expecting company."

"Uh, hi." Nadia tried to hide the book behind her.

Dameon laughed. "Okay. You know I saw what's in your hand, and I know why you're in my room."

"You do?" she asked.

"Let's see. Why would you two be in my room without permission?" He put a finger to his temple. "I don't know. Maybe because someone tried to convince you I was lying to you."

"Dameon, we know everything." Nadia's voice shook a tiny bit. It was so minor that Dameon may not have noticed, but I did. I noticed every little subtle detail with her.

"You don't know everything." Dameon shook his head. "If you did, you wouldn't be looking at me like that."

"Well, we know you've been hiding things." Her voice was strong now. She was pushing away her nerves. "And we know your name might not even be Dameon."

I decided to keep my mouth shut at first and let her take control of the conversation. She didn't like to feel like I doubted her.

Dameon shrugged. "Who isn't hiding things? And who cares what my name is?"

"Come on." I'd reached the end of my rope on keeping my mouth shut. He couldn't be serious.

"You knew the true story about Jackie." Nadia took a few steps toward him. "Yet you lied to us about it."

"No." He shook head. "No, I didn't lie. I withheld the truth. That's something altogether different. I had to do what I had to do." He took a seat on his bed. "I needed you guys on my side of things."

"So, you admit it. You were using us?"

"No, I was doing what was right. Just because Jackie only killed to protect a pup doesn't mean she didn't kill. It also doesn't mean the Elites aren't dangerous."

"But you're dangerous too." Nadia said exactly what I was thinking.

"Eventually, you'll have to choose a side in this. View it as the lesser of two evils if you want. Either way, you have to decide."

"Who says we have to?" I was so tired of all of it. "We're just students here."

"Today you are. But this is so much bigger than you."

"Don't we know it." Nadia sighed. "Listen. I have no idea who you really are or what you want."

"I want to stop the Elites. I want to keep things balanced." Dameon put a hand in his pocket. "Is that so hard to understand?"

"We don't know what to believe, but we are done trusting you blindly. We leave for break tomorrow. Are you even going to be back in the spring?" she asked.

"I'll be back if you don't blow my cover." He looked

between us. "But if you do, I'll just send someone else in my place." In a flash, he shifted into his wolf.

My wolf took over without warning and dove in front of Nadia, who was still standing in her human form. The ID and book had fallen to the floor.

Dameon picked up both with his mouth and jumped through the open window.

I jumped up on the windowsill ready to follow, but Nadia touched my back. My wolf loved the feel of her hand.

"What good is following him?" She kept her hand on me. "We know he's lying about something, and at least for now, he's gone. What else is there to do?" She removed her hand, and I shifted back to my human form.

Her eyes drank me in, and I smiled at her. "Glad you aren't so upset about seeing me naked anymore."

"Oh." She flushed. "Yeah. Did you want to go to the party?"

"I'm standing here naked after Dameon stole the evidence and jumped out the window, and you want to know if I want to go to the party?"

"Yes." She nodded. "That's exactly what I want to know."

"Sure." I felt a grin spread across my face. "That sounds like a great idea."

I knew I'd packed a dress for a reason. Thankfully, the black lace strapless dress fit well, because it was the only option I had. I put on some lipstick and a pair of heels. Ryan had been shocked by my sudden change of heart about taking a break, but I knew we needed it. Besides, what else could we do? We were stuck, living as pawns in some much bigger chess game we didn't fully understand. We had done our part for the time being, and it was time to focus on other things, namely us.

I didn't fully trust Jackie, but that didn't mean she was wrong about everything. We were only young once.

I took one more glance in the mirror before I headed out of my room and down into the central lounge. Ryan was dressed in a black suit that only made him look hotter than normal. Although, he always looked hot. No clothing could downplay it all that much.

"You look..." His eyes swept over me. "You look amazing, Nadia."

"So do you." I grinned at him. I didn't even care if I looked ridiculous doing it. I no longer worried about what Ryan thought of me. That was a huge step.

"Not like you." He put a hand around his neck. "You're breathtaking."

"If I knew it would get this reaction, I'd dress up more."

"You always look amazing. But that dress." His eyes were lidded, and I was even more glad I'd packed it.

He held out his arm. "Shall we?"

"Yes, we shall." I linked my arm with his and let him lead us down the stairs.

We walked outside to where the quad had been decorated for the occasion. There were bare lightbulbs hanging all over, and tables covered in bright colored table clothes that matched the different house colors scattered throughout and surrounding one large wooden dance floor. There were four big tables, all with a house's color covered in all sorts of foods. My eyes went immediately to the chocolate fountain off to the side of the dance floor that looked nearly empty even though there were dozens of people dancing.

"May I have this dance?" Ryan held out his arm right as the music switched to a slow song.

"I thought you'd never ask." I linked my arm with his and let him lead me onto the dance floor.

We danced closely together, barely dancing, because to do so would require creating more space between us.

Instead, we swayed, and I had absolutely no problem with that.

We danced for hours, to slow songs and fast ones, it didn't matter. And I knew I'd never get tired of being in his arms. As the night wore on I was holding on to him even tighter and resting my head on his chest.

"You ready to go?"

"Sure." I lifted my head from his chest. "That sounds great."

He wrapped his hand around mine and led me back toward the Wolf Born dorm. It was hard to believe we'd been at the academy for only one semester. So much had happened in the time there that it felt like so much more.

We passed Finn in the hall. "Hey, man. I'm out for the night." He winked at Ryan. At another time, that would have annoyed or terrified me. This time, it got me excited. Very excited.

Ryan unlocked his door, and we moved inside.

"I'm glad we went to the party." I slipped off my heels. Neither of us had specifically said anything about it, but I had no plans of going back to my room.

"Me too." He put his hands on my hips, the touch sending waves of awareness through me. "Mostly because I got to dance with you while you were wearing this dress."

"You like this dress a lot, huh?" I made a mental note to do some dress shopping when I was home on break.

"I'd like it a lot more if you weren't wearing it anymore though."

"Oh?" I fought the nerves welling deep inside. This was Ryan. I wanted this, and so did he.

"Yeah." He ran his lips down my neck. "I'd really like that."

He reached around and unzipped the back of my dress. It fell in a heap of black lace on the floor, leaving me in only a set of black bra and panties. I'd purposely chosen my only remotely sexy ones.

"Wow." Ryan's eyes slid over me. "You're even more gorgeous than I imagined."

"Well, you aren't done yet." I was feeling uncharacteristically bold, and I reached around and unclasped my bra. I let that fall to the floor. In an action so fast I didn't realize what was happening, his mouth was on my breast. I moaned as his teeth grazed my nipple.

"You like that, huh?" He looked up at me.

"Yeah, I do." I really, really liked it.

"You sure you're ready for this?" he asked. Didn't he realize the time to ask me that had come and gone?

"Yes, I'm ready." I wanted to be with him. I wanted to be fully connected with Ryan in a way I'd never wanted to connect with anyone before.

"Good." He slipped off his jacket and then moved on to his shirt. Once he was done, both had joined my dress and bra on the floor. He put my hands on his belt. I undid it and then unbuttoned his pants.

His lips crushed against mine as he slipped his hands into my panties, slowly slipping them off. I took him in my hand, marveling at his size and wondering how in the world this wouldn't hurt like hell.

I didn't need to worry. I was flying high by the time he laid me down on his bed. His fingers worked me expertly before he moved on top of me and looked into my eyes. "I love you. I love you so fucking much." He thrust into me, and my entire world changed.

I was still on a high from the magic of his fingers, but having him inside of me was an entirely new experience. It was nothing like I expected. It was everything.

He never stopped looking deep into my eyes, watching my reactions, needing to know that I was okay. I'd never felt safer in my life.

"Does this mean we're officially together?"

"We've been officially together since day one. I love you, Nadia Hazel, and I will always love you."

"I love you, Ryan Grayson." I put my arms around his neck.

"Just so you know, if we mate, you don't have to take the Grayson name."

"Thank you." I appreciated that he'd even offer that.

"And I'd even take Hazel as a name if you wanted."

"Wait. What?" I couldn't have heard him right.

He laughed. "Hey, then everyone will think I'm smarter."

I swatted at him.

"Or we could do Hazel-Grayson," he suggested.

"Hazel-Grayson. I like the sound of it." I ruminated. "Or just Grayson. I haven't decided yet."

"All I need you to decide is that, eventually, one day you'll be my mate." He brushed his lips against mine.

"I already made that decision."

"Then you have made me the happiest wolf ever." He kissed me hard.

I refused to interrupt the kiss, but I felt exactly the same way.

THANK YOU

Thank you for reading *Wolf Born*. We hope you enjoyed it! Please consider leaving an honest review at your point of purchase. Reviews help us in so many ways!

Stay up to date with the authors:

Visit Alyssa at https://www.alyssaroseivy.com

Stay up to date on Alyssa's new releases: ARI New Release Newsletter.

To see a complete list of Alyssa's books, please visit: http://www.alyssaroseivy.com/book-list-faq/

Visit Jennifer at https://jennifersnyderbooks.com

Stay up to date on Jennifer's new releases: Jennifer's Newsletter

To see a complete list of Jennifer's books please visit: https://jennifersnyderbooks.com/book-list/

The Lunar Academy continues with Wolf Blood, Year One !

Eager to find out more? The Lunar Academy continues in Wolf Blood, book two in year one. New House. New Couple. New Clue to the Mystery.

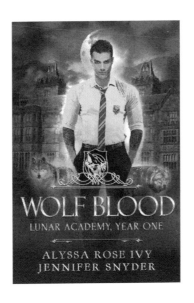

Four Houses. Traditions. Secrets. And Romance Waiting At Every Turn. Welcome to Lunar Academy. Which House Will You Choose?

Faith Brooks thinks of the academy as a new beginning. It's a way for her to put a traumatic event behind her and create a new life for herself. One where she understands her wolf as much as her vampire. And, one where she doesn't repeat past mistakes by falling for a guy who's unable to love. Too bad the academy doesn't teach students to tame their wild hearts as well as their wolves.

Axel Stone is a rough-around-the-edges, tattooed, bad boy. His fists are his only way at maintaining his sanity, but he's ready to learn more control over his demons. The academy is his ticket to learning how to find balance within himself and to keep a promise he made to someone he lost. No one will distract him from keeping that promise. Until he meets Faith.

Pulled together into the mysterious disappearance of a friend, the two discover the heart wants what the heart wants and love sometimes finds those who aren't looking.

Available now!